MURDER MOST PUZZLING

THE SECONDHAND WITCH COZY MYSTERIES - BOOK 3

FIONA SNYCKERS

Sign up to Fiona Snyckers' mailing list for special offers and information on new releases.

https://landing.mailerlite.com/webforms/landing/r4a9m8

A NOTE ON THE TEXT

This novel uses American spelling and idiom, conforming to Standard American English.

Chapter 1

*S*hrieks of laughter reverberated from the walls of Charmed Bookstore.

Luna Larkspur locked eyes with her barista and second-in-command, Harper Brave, and shook her head. "Rowdy lot, aren't they?"

"Tell me about it. They call themselves the Girl Talk book club, yeah? They should change their name to the Girl Giggles book club or the Girl Screams with Laughter book club." Harper stood on tiptoe to look over Luna's shoulder. "Now they've got into the Romance section and are reading each other extracts from the books." She handed Luna a bottle of white wine and a bottle of red wine. "Won't you go and top them up? I'm scared they'll eat me alive."

Grinning, Luna took the bottles over to the seven ladies and filled up their glasses. There were potato chips and other nibbles laid out in front of them, but Luna figured it was time to bring out the more substantial savory snacks to soak up some of that wine. She had spent the previous evening baking for just this occasion and had spinach and ricotta mini quiches and chicken puff pies ready to offer them.

Luna returned to the coffee station to pick up the quiches and pies that Harper had warmed for her. As she laid them out for the ladies, one of them looked up from her book.

"Thank you, my love. That looks delicious. It was such a great idea to move our book club meetings to Charmed."

The other ladies nodded like bobble-head dolls.

"Genius idea."

"Brilliant."

"*Such* an improvement."

"Just look at these delicious snacks."

"And we didn't have to lift a finger ourselves."

This provoked more giggling. The original speaker winked at Luna as though to say, *I told you so.* She was Detective Sergeant Melinda Knight – the most senior officer in command of Moonstone Island's tiny police force. Luna had only been living on the island a few months, but she and Melinda were already fast friends.

Luna tilted her head to check out the cover of the book Melinda was holding. "*Her Billionaire Kidnapper*? Now that's a classic of the genre."

"It's a hoot," said Melinda. "And strangely compelling too. I don't know if I'll be able to leave here tonight without buying it."

Her words were music to Luna's shopkeeper's soul.

One of the other ladies held up the book she was looking through. "This one's called *The Billionaire's Promise*. I didn't even know this was a genre."

"Oh, it's huge," said Luna. "Billionaire romances are one of the hottest selling sub-genres in contemporary romance."

"I can see why," said one of the ladies. "It's the ultimate

fantasy, isn't it? That some super-rich bloke will come along and sweep you away into a life of luxury."

The ladies made swoony "Ooooh" noises, but Melinda and Luna wore identical frowns.

"I'd still want to have my career," said the policewoman.

"Me too," said Luna. "I couldn't just do nothing all day."

"Oh, you wouldn't do nothing," said Melinda's friend. "You would be terribly busy entertaining the billionaire's clients, raising his children, and decorating his many houses for him."

"Sounds like hell, quite frankly," said Melinda, and Luna could only agree.

"I remember a time when millionaires were good enough to be the heroes of romance novels," Luna said. "Now they all have to be billionaires. That's inflation for you, right?"

The ladies laughed far louder than the mild joke warranted.

Luna curtseyed in acknowledgement and left them to their own devices. Back at the coffee station, she checked on the sweet snacks that she and Harper would serve with tea and coffee later in the evening. These consisted of Sugar-Crystal Cookies to Stimulate Concentration and Triple-Layer Brownies to Promote a Convivial Evening. Both were old family recipes that Luna had found in a recipe book that dated back generations in her family. She was doubting the brownies now. The ladies could use some concentration, but they needed no help in the conviviality department. If they got any more convivial, they would be swinging from the chandeliers.

"This was a good idea." Harper glanced at their guests and gave a satisfied nod. "Not only are we making a tidy profit on the venue fee, but you can bet they'll buy plenty of books by the end of the evening."

"That's what I'm hoping. You really didn't need to be here tonight, Harper," Luna said for the second time that day. "There are only seven of them. I can manage on my own, although admittedly it's nice to have your help."

"I wanted to do it, for two reasons." Harper counted them off on her fingers. "One, the overtime pay is very welcome. I'm pretty skint this month. And two, Mum is on a tear with her spring-cleaning. I had to clear out before I got drafted to wash the curtains or something horrible like that."

"It's October," Luna pointed out.

"I know, right? Mum's idea of getting a head start on her spring-cleaning is to do it in autumn. I decided I was safer here."

∿

Luna served tea and coffee at nine o'clock. Her baked goods came in for extensive praise. And unless she was much mistaken, the noise level rose even further, suggesting that the Conviviality Brownies were working.

As she topped up the milk jug, the tinkling of a mobile phone made her look up. It wasn't as common a sound as it had been a few years earlier. These days everyone, Luna included, seemed to keep their phones on silent. But there was one person whose phone was always on – one person who had to be reachable at all times.

Melinda scooped up her phone. "D.S. Knight?"

Apparently used to their friend's habit of receiving calls at odd hours, the ladies continued their conversation in lowered tones. Luna stayed in the vicinity, reshelving books and gathering plates. She had an uneasy feeling – a kind of prickle at the back of her neck – that told her all was not well. She glanced at Melinda's face, but it was unreadable.

Luna's cat seemed to share her unease because he hopped off Melinda's lap where he had been happily ensconced for the past hour and came to stretch his front paws up the side of Luna's leg. She bent down and picked him up, whereupon he settled into her arms purring like a large and furry jackhammer.

She stroked him, deriving as much comfort from his presence as he was from hers.

His name was Pyewacket and he was a seal-point Siamese who had originally belonged to Luna's late grandfather. Luna had inherited the cat along with Charmed Book Store several months earlier. He was a wise and empathetic animal with a strong streak of mischief. Luna loved him very much.

Melinda slipped her phone into her bag and stood up. "I'm afraid I have to go, girls. There's been an incident at the Scout Hall. This will probably take a while so don't expect me back."

Since incidents on Moonstone Island usually consisted of parking disputes, minor neighborly feuds, and cases of littering or loitering, none of the ladies appeared alarmed. They settled more comfortably into their chairs and picked up the wineglasses that they had temporarily abandoned in favor of tea.

"Bye then," said one of the ladies. "We'll message you when we've decided on a date for next month."

"Do you want any of those?" asked another, indicating the small pile of Billionaire romances Melinda had accumulated next to her chair.

"Oh, yes I do, thanks. Won't one of you pay for them and

I'll pay you back when I come and pick them up tomorrow. Got to run now."

As Melinda hurried to the exit, she locked eyes with Luna and gave a slight but unmistakable sideways jerk of the head.

Luna let her out the front door which had been locked to discourage anyone from wondering in. Then she hurried over to Harper who was stacking the small dishwasher Luna had recently acquired.

"Can you hold the fort, Harper? Melinda wants me to go with her to the Scout Hall."

Harper looked thoughtful. "Does she though? Must be serious."

"I'm afraid you're right. She only calls me in for important matters."

Harper waved a dishcloth at her. "Off you go then. I'll stay until these ladies leave and clean up afterwards. Then I'll lock up behind me."

"Thanks, Harper. You're a life saver. See you tomorrow." Luna hurried out of the bookstore in Melinda's wake.

Her friend was so far ahead of her that she had to jog to catch up.

"What's up?" she asked, as she pulled up puffing next to Melinda. She really needed to work out more.

"I'm not entirely sure. According to Arthur, they found a body at the Jigsaw Puzzle Convention." Police Constable Arthur Cooper was one of Melinda's colleagues.

"A Jigsaw Puzzle Convention? Is that a thing?"

"Apparently. It's taking place at the Scout Hall over the next three or four days. Tonight was supposed to be the opening ceremony. I don't know how far they had got with it when this happened."

Luna trotted to keep up with Melinda's long strides as

she turned up a side road in the direction of the High Street where the Scout Hall was located just a block down from the Village Hall.

"Did P.C. Cooper tell you who the dead person was?" she asked.

"All I know is that it's a man and that no one seems to recognize him."

"Must be from somewhere else. Everyone knows everyone else on this island, except me, and that's just because I'm new."

"Very likely," Melinda agreed. "This Jigsaw Puzzle Convention was expected to attract visitors from all over, including from other countries. He might be anyone. I just hope we can get him ID'd as quickly as possible. Otherwise we'll be working in the dark."

"Why didn't you want your book club friends to know that there was a dead body involved?"

"The person might have died of natural causes. I don't want to start any rumors about a murder that might turn out not to be true."

"Makes sense."

The Scout Hall was no more than a hundred feet ahead of them. It was clear that something had happened. All the lights were blazing, and people milled around outside. Faint strains of classical music could be heard emanating from the building. As they approached, this cut off.

P.C. Cooper hurried towards them. "Thank goodness you're here, ma'am. Please come quickly."

Chapter 2

P.C. Cooper nodded at Luna as Melinda hurried ahead into the Scout Hall.

"Evening, Luna. I'm not surprised that the boss called you in on this one. It's tricky, all right."

"You don't think it's natural causes then?"

"Not if thirty years as a police officer have taught me anything. You'll see."

Luna shivered. She had no desire to see. Solving a mystery as a kind of intellectual puzzle was one thing, but being in the presence of an actual dead body was another. It was not something she could be unemotional about, or something she ever wanted to get used to.

PC Cooper led his boss straight to the body, but Luna hung back to get an impression of her surroundings. She was already familiar with the Scout Hall. It was a large and drafty space, much used as a center of village life. A steady stream of clubs and societies met there on a weekly or monthly basis. The west wall featured a community notice board where people could put up flyers for free. Luna had used it herself on a number of occasions.

Right now, the hall was filled with dozens of colorful stalls and tables advertising merchandise and events connected to the world of jigsaw puzzles. Most of the stalls were still functioning, but it was clear that people already knew something was wrong. The four exit doors of the hall had been closed and were guarded by police officers. People talked on their phones, tapped out text messages, and engaged in whispered conversations with each other.

As Luna watched, the scene-of-crime officers arrived, accompanied by the local doctor who usually served as the coroner and medical examiner.

Tearing herself away from her contemplation of the hall, Luna followed the SOCOs into a corridor that seemed to lead to a set of administrative offices. A small group of people were standing around looking at the body on the floor. Only two of them, as far as Luna could see, had any business being there – and that was PC Cooper and Melinda.

The person on the floor was lying face up in a sprawled position. Luna caught a glimpse of his face before squeezing her eyes shut and turning away. The only thing she knew for sure was that she had never seen him before.

"Does anyone know this man?" Melinda asked. "Does anyone recognize him?"

None of the onlookers replied.

Luna glanced from face to face. Some displayed horror and some open curiosity, while others were pale with shock. One face caught her eye in particular. It belonged to a small, mousy woman with prematurely grey hair, wearing a long skirt and a high-necked shirt. As Luna looked at her face, it was as though a palimpsest were being imposed over her features.

As Luna watched, a shadowy image seemed to waver

into focus, as though it had been superimposed over the woman's face. It was the face of the dead man.

"She does," Luna blurted, pointing at the woman. "She knows who he is."

Melinda turned to look at the woman. "Is that true? Do you know who this man is?"

The woman blinked rapidly, her gaze flicking between Luna and Melinda. "But how ... how ...?"

"You look alike," said Luna. This wasn't really true, but she had seen something in that palimpsest moment that told her these two people were related.

As the woman dithered, Melinda made her voice stern. "This is serious, ma'am. If you know who this man is, I need you to tell me his name and how you know him."

The woman seemed to be on the verge of tears. "His ... his name is Paul Robard. He was ... he was my brother."

"I'm very sorry for your loss," said Melinda.

"So he's ... he's definitely dead then?"

"I'm afraid so, yes. I'll need to speak to you, please. Did anyone else here know Mr. Robard?"

The onlookers shook their heads. Melinda quirked an eyebrow at Luna. When Luna gave a tiny nod, she turned to PC Cooper and asked him to clear away the onlookers.

"All except you," Melinda said, indicating the sister of the deceased. "We need to make room for the scene-of-crime officers and the medical examiner now. Please follow me into this vacant office, ma'am. You too, Luna," she added as her friend tried to slip away.

"Can I join you in, like, ten minutes?" asked Luna. "I just want to take a wander around the hall." Her eyes beseeched Melinda.

"Oh, all right. But get back in here soon, please."

Making the most of her opportunity, Luna scuttled back

out into the hall. The exit doors were still locked and PC Cooper and the junior officers under him were moving from person to person, taking down their statements and full details. Luna estimated that it would take them a couple of hours to get through everyone. That was what murder did – it disrupted the lives of everyone in the vicinity. There was no doubt in her mind that it had been murder. Her brief glimpse of the victim had told her that he had been struck from behind by a heavy object. She would have expected him to have fallen forward in that case, but perhaps someone had rolled him onto his back after the fact.

Operating on instinct, Luna took out her phone and activated the camera. She knew how unreliable human memory was, and hers in particular. It was always useful to memorialize things, even if you were convinced you would remember them later.

Keeping her eye on the time, she moved around the hall, snapping pictures of every stall and table and what was displayed on them. She tried to get as many faces of the people involved as possible.

One stall in particular gave her pause. More than that, it sent a chill down her spine.

The stall had a myths and legends theme, featuring some beautifully painted jigsaw puzzles. Luna's eyes glided over the Norse gods and the Greek and Roman legends, and landed on a sign that said *The Magic of Moonstone Island*. This section featured puzzles designed around a geography of the island and some of its more well-known landmarks, like the pier that jutted out to sea, the church in the High Street, and the cliffs on the eastern side of the island. Some of the puzzles included symbols of magic and mysticism. What caught Luna's eye was a series of five-hundred-piece puzzles depicting ancient and curiously carved wooden objects with symbols engraved on them. The series was called *The Glyphs of Moonstone Island*.

Just looking at them made her feel as though spiders were crawling up and down her arms. She had to remind herself that the glyphs were a common part of island lore. There was no need to be suspicious of the stall for selling their likeness, nor of the owner of the stall. Nevertheless, she took careful photographs of the puzzles and of the two people running the stall.

When she felt as though she had documented the hall to her satisfaction, she hurried back to the admin offices to sit in on Melinda's interview with the sister of the dead man. She picked her way past the medical examiner and the SOCOs and knocked on the door.

"Come in," said Melinda. "Oh, it's you, Luna. Miss Kitson, this is Luna Larkspur, a local business owner who sometimes consults to the Moonstone Island Police Force. Luna, this is Tina Kitson, sister of the late Mr. Robard."

"My condolences on the loss of your brother," said Luna.

Tina Kitson nodded, staring at the floor. When she raised her eyes, her face was distressed. "Thank you. I mean … the thing is, we didn't actually know each other."

Luna glanced at Melinda as she sat down. It was clear that this part of the story was known to her.

"So you didn't grow up together?" Luna asked.

Tina looked at the floor again. "No."

"May I ask if you were half siblings?"

Tina shifted in her seat. "No. Full siblings. Same mother, same father."

"How did it come about that you didn't know each other?"

Tina took a deep breath. Luna sensed genuine pain in her. "Two years before I was born, my parents found out that they were expecting a child. They had been married for a few years already, but weren't in the financial position that they had hoped to be in before starting a family. My mother would have had to return to work after the baby was born and she really wanted to be a stay-at-home mum. Also, they were hoping to move into a bigger house ..." Tina tailed off.

"I see," said Luna, although she wasn't sure that she did.

"So, what they did is ... they decided to have the baby and give it up for adoption. It wasn't the right time for them to have a child and they knew there were many couples who were desperate to adopt."

"Did they go through an agency?"

"Yes, they contacted a number of private adoption agencies and registered with them. They were shown profiles of people wanting to adopt and they chose a couple that they thought would be best suited to raise the child."

Out of the corner of her eye, Luna saw Melinda making a note.

"I'm sure they were very careful in the choice they made," she said, trying to keep Tina talking.

"They were ... or at least, they thought they were. Remember, this was forty-seven years ago. My brother was born and immediately taken away from my mother. She didn't get to hold him even for a moment. He was given straight to the adoptive parents, and they took him away. It was a closed adoption, which means that my parents opted not to know the identity of the adoptive couple, beyond the facts contained in the original profile. They chose to make it impossible for the baby ever to trace them, even as an adult."

"Weren't those laws changed?" asked Melinda.

"Yes. That's how I managed to trace him. But at the time,

my parents thought they were safe. He would never come back into their lives.

Luna thought that was an interesting choice of words. "How did you find out that he existed?"

Tina's face twisted. "Oh, my parents were very open about it. When I was about four years old, they sat me down and told me about the older brother who now lived with some other family. They emphasized how much they had wanted me when my mother was expecting and how happy they were when I was born. I think they were trying to make me feel 'special' or 'chosen' or something."

"Was that not how you felt?" Luna asked as her story trailed off again.

"No. Even as a small child, I realized that it was just a matter of timing that had made my parents decide to keep me. There was nothing special about me. If I had been born two years earlier, I would have been the one who was given up for adoption. It made me feel like I was there on sufferance. Like I had to behave myself all the time or they might change their minds about keeping me."

Chapter 3

*A*n uncomfortable silence descended.

Luna thought, not for the first time, how awkward, messy, and painful this business of being human was. She was relieved when Melinda took over the questioning.

"So, you and your brother made contact in adulthood?"

Tina squeezed her eyes shut for a moment. Then she blurted out, "I just want to say that I respect everyone's rights to create their family however they want. I'm not saying my parents did anything wrong. I'm just saying it was ... difficult for me."

Melinda kept her voice gentle. "No one is judging here. We only want to find out what happened."

"Okay. Well." Tina pulled herself together. "I was allowed to access the records of my brother's adoption. I only went looking for them when I was past thirty and thinking about having children of my own. His current last name didn't match the name of the couple that had originally adopted him, but the paper trail said that he was the right person. I sent a letter and then an email, but I got no reply. I figured he wasn't interested in making contact with his birth family."

"Were your parents involved in these attempts to get in touch?" asked Melinda.

"No. I never told them what I was doing. I know they would have hated the thought."

"What happened next?"

"I left it alone for more than fifteen years. Then, a few months ago, I decided to try again. I wrote a letter and an email to the same addresses I'd been given. He replied to the email. He wasn't exactly enthusiastic, but he agreed to meet me. The problem was, I live in London, and he is apparently based in Yorkshire."

Even Luna, with her fuzzy knowledge of the geography of the UK, knew that this was an inconvenient distance.

"What did you do then?" asked Melinda.

"Nothing for a few months. I was willing to travel up to Yorkshire to see him, but he kept throwing obstacles in the way. Then he said that he was coming to Moonstone Island in October for this jigsaw puzzle convention. It was easy enough for me to take the train to Brighton and hop on a ferry to come here. We were going to meet for the first time at the opening ceremony."

"You were *going* to meet?" asked Melinda. "Does that mean you didn't get the opportunity to do so?"

Tina stared at the floor before answering. "We had exchanged photographs, so I knew what he looked like. I saw him across the hall at about eight o'clock this evening, but he was deep in conversation with someone at one of the stalls. Then I lost sight of him. The next time I saw him, he was ..." She shuddered. "He was lying over there. So you see, I wasn't lying when I said that I didn't know him. And now I never will." A tear rolled down her cheek.

～

As Melinda continued to question Tina about her brother, she indicated to Luna that she could go home. The rest of the evening would consist of routine police work. Luna knew she would still be involved, even if it was only as a sounding board for her friend, but for tonight she was done.

She arrived back at the bookstore to find that Harper had cleared everything up and locked the door behind her on her way out. Luna greeted the cat with a stroke and traipsed up the stairs to the tiny apartment she occupied above the bookstore.

It was almost midnight, but she took a few minutes to pay attention to the many potted herbs and edible plants that hung in tiers from her ceiling. She nipped off dead leaves, watered any plants that were dry, and added minerals and salts to the soil that needed it. Not all the plants belonged to her. Three were what she liked to think of as guests or, more accurately, patients.

Word had got around on the island that Luna was the person to call if you needed to revive any pot plants that were struggling. Her success rate was high. Sometimes it took a few days and sometimes it took weeks, but she hadn't lost a patient yet.

As Luna worked, she chattered away to the cat about the events of the evening – the success of Melinda's book-club event and the interview with Tina Kitson. Anyone listening would have written her off as a crazy cat lady. But the thing about Pyewacket was that he listened politely, without a hint of judgment.

"It was *such* a sad story," Luna said about Tina. "I really felt sorry for her."

The cat made a noise that sounded like, "*prrp*".

"She seems to have grown up feeling really insecure, as though her parents could change their minds about wanting her at any moment."

Pyewacket blinked slowly at her.

"Was she the one who hit her brother over the head? Or was it the person she saw him talking to earlier? Or someone else entirely? Melinda will have her work cut out trying to figure out that one."

Luna met the cat's eyes and shrugged. "Yes, yes. Of course I will help out as much as I can. If Melinda wants me to."

The cat made a skeptical noise.

"No, I don't know where to start. Maybe I'll pay a visit to the Scout Hall tomorrow at lunch time to see how the Jigsaw Puzzle Convention is progressing. That wouldn't be meddling, would it?"

The cat sighed and hopped pointedly onto the bed. He seemed to suggest that she should hurry up and come to bed. But when she finally slipped under the duvet, he stood bolt upright, puffed out his tail like a giant pipe cleaner, and galloped around the apartment as though he were being chased by demons. Then Luna heard the church clock chiming midnight and it all made sense.

The witching hour.

This wasn't the first time she had noticed her cat going crazy at this time of night. She was mostly asleep for it, but when she did manage to catch the show, it was an impressive whirlwind of shadow boxing, steeple chasing, and acrobatics.

As the sound of the last chime died away, he hopped back on the bed and began to wash himself as though nothing had happened.

Luna tickled his chin. "Ridiculous animal."

She felt physically tired, but her mind was too unsettled for sleep. She rummaged in the pile of books on her nightstand and came up with the Diary of Coco Larkspur. Written out by hand a hundred years earlier, it was the diary of Luna's great-great-grandmother who had moved to Moonstone Island in the 1920s to take over the family business – Charmed Bookstore. Luna hadn't read the diary from cover to cover, but liked to dip into it from time to time because it was full of wisdom and insight that she often found helpful. Coco had made a name for herself as a healer, a wise woman, and an expert in plant life.

Luna opened the diary at random and paged through it until a passage caught her eye.

What to do when your sympathies are engaged

Sometimes you will find yourself attempting to solve a mystery where your sympathies are overly engaged with one or other of the people involved. This person may have had a hard life or have endured circumstances that tug at your heart strings.

I would advise caution in this case.

I would never for one moment suggest that you try to suppress your emotions as a Larkspur woman. Much of your intuition and insight comes from your ability to imagine yourself in someone else's position and to feel sympathy for them. But this can be taken too far.

If you feel an excess of sympathy for someone, it can blind you to their faults and cause you to overlook something important. It is a difficult balancing act.

I would advise you to put your sympathies to one side as you

*look coolly at the situation and apply logic and a balance of prob-
abilities in solving the problem.*

*Your emotion should be a tool that assists you rather than a
blindfold that prevents you from seeing clearly.*

Luna nodded. As always, consulting with Coco had a
calming effect on her. She yawned hugely and her eyelids
drooped. She fell asleep as she so often did, with a book
lying open on her chest.

~

Luna over-slept after her late night, only waking up at
seven-thirty. She had to rush through her morning routine
in order to open the coffee-serving hatch promptly at eight
o'clock. The rest of the bookstore opened at nine, but Luna
served takeaway coffee and home-baked cookies to the early
morning crowd from eight onwards.

That hour before Harper joined her at nine o'clock to
take over barista duties was often the busiest of Luna's day.
She wasn't as fast or as skilled as Harper when it came to
coffee-making. But at that hour of the morning, people
mostly wanted their coffee with the minimum waiting time.
They didn't care about having fancy patterns drawn in the
foam of their cappuccinos. Harper would flex those skills
later for the tourists.

The tourist trade wasn't as busy as it had been in the
summer, but Moonstone Island still attracted a steady
stream of day-trippers, drawn by the picturesque village, an
eclectic mix of shops, and of course the pier, with its
endlessly pinging arcade games and casino – a big draw
card.

At this hour of the morning, the sun was low in the sky, its feeble rays just starting to touch the western side of the island. As it rose higher, its glow would give the air the pearlescent sheen that the island was famous for. It was an atmospheric trick – a combination of sun and clouds and the reflection from the sea that gave the island its glow.

But right now, it was gloomy out there and most of the customers Luna served had their grumpy, Monday morning faces on.

"Morning, Luna!" a voice trilled.

"Morning, Viola. What can I get for you?"

Viola Harlow was the owner of Vintage Viola, a delightful store in the covered market. She was a notable exception to the grumpy face rule. Viola was always smiling and friendly – a naturally charismatic person.

"A vanilla bean latte, please, darling child. With chocolate sprinkles on top."

"Coming right up." Luna adjusted the settings on the coffee machine and set Viola's coffee going. "You seem cheerful today – even more so than usual."

"Oh, I am. I have an old friend coming to visit. She hasn't been to the island in months. We've both been too busy. It'll be lovely to see her."

"I hope you both have a good time." Luna handed Viola her coffee and tried to pass her the change.

Viola waved it away. "Pop it in the tip jar, sweetie. We might see you later if our caffeine levels drop to a dangerous low." She departed with a wink and a wave.

Luna worked steadily until nine. She tried not to think about how nice it would be to have an old friend visiting her. The problem with leaving home and moving to the other side of the Atlantic was that you left your friends and family behind. Social media and video calling were great ways to stay in touch, but there were people she missed. At least she was going home for Thanksgiving next month. And she was forging new friendships here on the island.

Luna looked up and smiled as Harper came rushing up, her newly purple hair streaming out behind her.

"I'm not late!" she said.

Chapter 4

*L*una stepped aside to let Harper take over the barista duties. "You're not late at all. There's the church clock striking nine. I like your hair, by the way."

Harper waved this away. "Never mind that now. I want to know what happened at the Scout Hall last night. Did someone really die?"

"I'm afraid so. His name was Paul Robard. He lived in Yorkshire and was here for the Jigsaw Puzzle Convention."

"Did he just drop dead, or did someone kill him?"

"He was attacked. Someone hit him on the back of the head with something hard."

"Who?"

"That," said Luna, "is the million-dollar question. No one seems to have witnessed it. His long-lost sister saw him talking to someone at one of the stalls earlier in the evening. Then he disappeared and the next time she saw him he was dead. They were going to meet for the first time last night, but never got the opportunity."

Harper blinked. "That's so sad."

"Yes, it is. Assuming she's telling the truth, of course."

"What does Jim think?" Harper looked over Luna's shoulder in the direction of the Permanent Collection – a reference section of the bookstore that was open to members of the public for research purposes.

"I don't know. He's not here yet."

"That's odd. He usually arrives at nine, same as me."

Luna shrugged. "Maybe he's not coming in today."

It was a disappointing thought, although she wasn't about to admit that to anyone. Jim Cooke was the bookstore's tame academic who spent most days conducting research in the Permanent Collection. Based at Oriel College, Oxford, he had occasional lecturing and tutoring duties, but spent most of his time in Charmed researching his current book.

Luna shook her head. It was time to put Jim Cooke out of her mind.

"Can you hold the fort for a while?" she asked Harper. "I want to take a look at the Jigsaw Puzzle Convention."

"Of course. You go ahead."

Luna shrugged herself into a lightweight jacket and stepped out of the bookstore. The gentle, pearly weather of earlier had turned into a blustery fall day with the icy promise of colder weather to follow. She trudged up Seagull Lane towards the High Street, following the same route she and Melinda had taken the night before.

The Scout Hall looked strangely ordinary in the dull light of day. The night before it had been lit up like a Christmas tree. Now all the doors were closed against the gusting wind. Only one door stood ajar, suggesting that day one of the convention had got underway at nine o'clock, as scheduled. Luna noticed P.C. Cooper and Melinda's vehicles parked in the street, suggesting that they were in the vicinity.

"*See?*" A voice in her head seemed to say. "*The police are already here. They're on the job. And they're competent officers. There's no reason for you to interfere. You should go back to the store and carry on with your cataloguing.*"

Luna shook her head. She was going to ignore that little voice. First of all, she could never resist a mystery. Secondly, she knew she could be useful to the investigation. Melinda knew it too, which was why she had invited Luna along the night before. And thirdly, even if she could do no good, she would be careful not to do any harm.

Luna hurried across the street and let herself into the hall, closing the door behind her. It was warmer inside than out, but only marginally. The Scout Hall was a notoriously drafty space.

The events of the night before didn't seem to have put a damper on the convention. If possible, even more stalls were crammed into the hall that morning. The doors had only been open a short while, but a respectable number of browsers already wandered between the tables, with more coming in every minute. The hall was filled with a quiet roar of conversation.

Luna hoped that not too many people remembered her as the person who had come in with the police the night before. She wanted to be as anonymous as possible as she wandered around asking questions. Most of the people in the hall were from somewhere else. Luna had lived in the village long enough to be able to tell an islander from a visitor.

She stood near the entrance and tried to imagine herself as Tina, newly arrived from the ferry, and looking anxiously about to spot her long-lost brother. She would walk a few steps into the hall, Luna imagined, rather than hanging back in the door-way. Luna could almost feel the surge of excitement that would have pushed her through the crowds as she scanned faces for the features of the relative that she had never met in person.

Luna's heart began to thunder as she opened herself up more and more to the trace energies of the night before.

Where was he? Where was he? She could hardly believe the day was finally here. After all those years of imagining what he would be like, her curiosity was about to be satisfied. All those years she had played imaginary games with him as a child, all those times she had dreamed about him, all those times she had imagined herself being in his shoes – it all led up to this moment.

There he was! She felt it like a blow to the chest. In photographs, she could see a sibling resemblance between them. In person, he looked shockingly like her father. Their father. Even the way he spoke and the gestures he made were the same.

He hadn't noticed her yet.

He was deep in conversation with a man in a tweed jacket with brown leather patches on the elbows. The man's face was turned away from her but that gave her more opportunity to study her brother's face.

The conversation between the two men seemed too vociferous to be entirely friendly. She was reluctant to interrupt. She would stand there and wait to be noticed, just as she had her whole life.

Anger exploded inside her as unexpectedly as a sucker punch. Where had it come from? Was it watching him make the same gestures as her father – adopt the same mannerisms as he spoke, even though they had never met? She had to look away and get herself under control. And when she glanced up again, he was gone.

Luna blinked hard in an effort to free herself from this glimpse into the past. As she looked around, she realized that it was morning, not evening, and that Paul Robard was not standing in front of her. Her knees felt weak.

She tried to rationalize what had happened

It was no more than speculation, of course – a kind of imaginative recreation of what Tina might have been thinking and feeling. But it had felt like more than that. It had felt like a vision.

Luna shoved this thought to the back of her mind where it took up residence alongside a number of other disconcerting experiences. She liked living in the real world. There was a limit to the amount of weirdness she was prepared to deal with.

At least she now knew exactly where Paul Robard had been standing when his sister saw him. It was a stall that specialized in puzzles with an architectural theme. They were glossy and detailed, with excellent color values and nuance. Luna recognized at a glance the Parthenon, the Colosseum, the Moonstone Island Church, and a domed building that she thought might have been the Bodleian Library at Oxford. There were also more detailed puzzles depicting specific architectural features like Corinthian columns, gargoyles, and vaulted ceilings.

And there was a man in a tweed jacket at the stall.

As Luna hurried over, she saw that it was more of a regular sports coat than a tweed jacket. She also realized that she recognized the wearer.

"Jim."

He turned at the sound of her voice. "Luna. Hello. Have you come to scold me for playing hooky from the permanent collection?"

The curse of being a redhead was how easily one blushed. "Oh, weren't you in this morning? I ... didn't notice."

"Are you also a fan of jigsaw puzzles?"

"Not really. I haven't done one since I was a child. Once I mastered a forty-piece puzzle my kindergarten teacher called it a day and let me read books instead, which is what I wanted to do in the first place. Do you enjoy puzzles?"

Out of the corner of her eye, Luna noticed a man slide in behind the tables of the stall and take up his position there. She also noticed that he had on a tweed jacket with leather patches at the elbows.

"Jigsaw puzzles are a family tradition for us," said Jim. "Especially at Christmas time when we usually have an elaborate five-thousand-piece puzzle on the go. My mother and sister are the true fanatics in the family. I'm more of a dabbler. I was hoping to find some puzzles for them as gifts."

Luna leaned towards Jim and lowered her voice. "You heard what happened here last night?"

Jim didn't reply. He just inclined his head slightly.

"Good. Then help me question this guy."

That was the great thing about Jim Cooke, Luna knew. You didn't have to spell anything out for him. His agile mind adjusted itself to new situations. He didn't flinch at being told to help her question the person manning the stall. He just stood by and awaited developments.

Luna raised her voice. "But darling, I don't *want* a puzzle of a boring building. I want to go back to the true crime display. Murderers through the ages!" She gave a delighted shiver.

Jim swung into action. "And I already told you, darling, that we can only afford one ten-thousand-piece puzzle. I like these architectural ones. It will be fun for both of us."

Luna pouted. "You mean it will be fun for you. I want to go back to the murderers."

The man in the tweed jacket cleared his throat. "Can I perhaps be of assistance? You say you're looking for a ten-thousand-piece puzzle? We have a very fine selection."

Jim sighed. "The problem is that my wife and I have such different tastes. I like old buildings and she likes anything with a true-crime theme."

"Let's go back to the murderers," Luna whined.

Reluctant to lose the sale, the man selected some puzzle boxes and laid them on the table for their inspection. "If you're interested in true crime, this scene of Victorian London shows several of the sites where Jack the Ripper committed his murders."

Luna leaned forward, as though reluctantly interested. "That's not bad."

"I heard someone died here last night," said Jim. "Right here in this hall."

Luna shrugged as she looked at the Victorian London puzzle. "I saw that on the internet, but it seemed to be from natural causes."

They looked appealingly at the man. His shrug was awkward. "I can't say for sure, but there was a large police presence here last night. More than you would expect to find if someone died of natural causes. They were questioning everyone too."

Luna allowed herself to look a little interested. "Who was the dead man? Did you know him?"

Chapter 5

*T*he man shrugged. "The police asked me that too. I told them I'd never seen him before in my life. I believe his name has been released in the media this morning, but it didn't mean anything to me."

Luna scrolled through her phone. "Oh, yes. Here it is. Paul Robard. There's even a photograph of him." She held her phone up for Jim and the man to look at. "Surely you must have seen him last night?"

The man opened his mouth and then closed it again. He shook his head. "I don't think so, no."

Luna's pout increased. "This is so boring. Let's go back to the true crime stall. I bet they would have noticed something."

Jim rolled his eyes. "Just as you like, darling."

"Wait." The man held his hand out for her phone. "Let me have another look at him. He stared at the screen for a moment before nodding. "Okay, yes. I did speak to him last night."

Luna clasped her hands to her chest and squealed. "Did you really?" She turned to Jim. "Did you hear that, darling?

He actually spoke to the murdered man last night. Oh, this is so exciting. We can definitely buy a puzzle from here if you like."

"If you say so, my love."

"What did he say?" asked Luna.

The man frowned. "He was a bit of a nuisance, actually. First, he made me take out all my five-thousand-piece puzzles and show them to him. Then he pounced on one like it was a long-lost friend and said that he would take it. But when I tried to ring up the sale, his card was declined. He gave me another card and that was declined too. He kept insisting that it was some kind of technical error and that it was my card machine that was at fault rather than his bank account that was empty."

"Card machines do fail sometimes," said Jim.

"Yes, but not in this case. I rang up two other sales while this was going on and they went through perfectly. And it's not like the machine was giving me an error message. It said 'insufficient funds' as clear as day. It couldn't have been more obvious what was going on."

"What happened then?" asked Luna.

"I asked if he would prefer to pay cash, but he said he didn't have enough on him. So then I offered to keep the puzzle aside while he went to an ATM to draw money. There's one in the High Street, less than a block away. But he didn't like that idea either."

"It sounds like he simply couldn't afford it," said Jim. "Which is hardly your problem, right?"

The man huffed out a breath. "Exactly. And so I kept telling him. But he insisted that he had to have this puzzle. I even gave him my card with my website on it so he could order the puzzle when his finances were in better shape. But, no. It had to be this exact puzzle, right now. I offered to let him take a photo of the box but that wasn't good enough either. It was the actual puzzle pieces inside that he wanted."

Luna looked at him wide-eyed. "That's so strange. Did he say why he wanted them?"

"No. If you ask me, the man was unhinged. You'll never believe what he did next. He offered to pay me by check. Like I'm supposed to accept a personal check from a man who clearly doesn't have the funds to cover it. And he had the cheek to act as though I was insulting him by refusing."

"Then what happened?"

"I'm afraid I got a little testy with him. And he replied in kind. We had quite an argument going for a few minutes. Then I noticed that it was putting people off and probably costing me sales. So I called a halt to the whole thing and told him I wasn't going to bandy words with him any longer. I asked him please to step away from my stall and he did so. That was the last time I saw him."

Luna batted her eyelashes at him. "That's an amazing story."

"Which puzzle was it that he was so interested in?" asked Jim.

The man reached under the table and pulled out a box. "This one. It's a scene of the Moonstone Village High Street from the 1920s, as you can see. There's a fascinating mix of architecture in the buildings."

"Can we get this one, darling?" Luna begged. "It's like a real-life piece of true crime history." She giggled. "If you consider what happened last night to be history."

Then she caught sight of the price tag and nearly choked. "Two hundred and eighty pounds? Really?"

The man sniffed. "Yes, and that's discounted. This is a hand-made, artisanal wooden jigsaw puzzle from a limited edition of six. It has been discounted from three hundred pounds because, as you can see, there is some wear and tear to the box and some of the pieces have previously been handled. But it is nevertheless a collector's piece."

"Oh, please, darling!" she begged Jim. "I really, really want it."

With a show of reluctance, Jim took out his wallet and handed over two hundred and eighty pounds in cash. Then Luna held open a cloth shopping bag and allowed the man to slide the box into it. He slipped one of his business cards into the bag too. According to it, his name was Mr. Marcus Blackstone. His business was Blackstone's Puzzles.

"Thank you so much, Mr. Blackstone," said Luna. "I am absolutely thrilled with it."

Luna tucked her hand into Jim's arm and led him out of the hall. The moment they were outside, she disengaged herself and stepped politely away from him. "Great work, *darling*. You're an excellent co-conspirator."

"Thanks." Jim couldn't help looking pleased with himself. Then he stared at her. "Um, Luna? I don't mean to alarm you, but why is your shopping bag glowing?"

Luna looked down and almost dropped the bag. It was indeed glowing, and not in a good way.

Luna put the bag down on the sidewalk and backed up several steps. "Is it ... is it radioactive?"

"I don't think so. No, look. It's stopped glowing." Jim stepped up to the bag and peered inside. He saw a puzzle box, a printed receipt, and a business card. "It seems fine. Must have been a trick of the light." He picked up the bag and handed it back to Luna.

But the moment she took it, the bag started to glow again. This time she did drop it. "What on earth ...?"

Jim looked thoughtful. Luna could almost see the gears

turning in his head. "Okay, so my powerful intellect is telling me that the common factor in this weirdness is you. The bag didn't glow when Mr. Marcus Blackstone held it. It doesn't glow when it is on the ground. And it doesn't glow when I pick it up. It only glows when you hold it. There's a connection between you and it."

"It's my regular shopping bag. I use it to carry groceries home from Brave's Kwikmart. I can categorically state that it has never glowed before."

"Not between you and the shopping bag," said Jim. "There's a connection between you and the puzzle."

Luna folded her arms across her chest. First there had been that weird vision and now this. All she wanted was a normal life. "Well, I'm not walking all the way home carrying what looks like a miniature sun. People will point and stare. Please can you carry it."

Jim scooped up the shopping bag. It remained reassuringly unglowy. "There. Happy now?"

Luna smiled and fell into step beside him. "Delighted."

∼

"So, what did you make of our Mr. Marcus Blackstone?" Jim asked as they walked back to Charmed Bookstore.

"I'm not too sure. It's not that I don't believe the story he told us, but I can't help wondering why he wasn't honest with the police from the beginning. He seems to have brushed them off and pretended that he had never spoken to Paul Robard. He only told us the truth because we dangled a big sale in front of him."

"I can understand why he wasn't more forthcoming," said Jim. "First of all, he might very well have been the last person to speak to the victim before his death. And their conversation was an argument. It makes sense that he wouldn't want to draw suspicion to himself like that."

"That's true," Luna agreed.

"And secondly, some people don't want to cooperate with the authorities. They're afraid of getting drawn into something that is going to complicate their lives. So, their response is to give the police the brush-off. They pretend that they saw and heard nothing."

Luna had to acknowledge that this was also true. Over the past few months, she had worked so closely with the local police that it was easy to forget that not everyone felt the same way.

The sight of Jim swinging the shopping bag as he walked reminded her of something. She pulled out her wallet and extracted two hundred and eighty pounds. "Here you go, 'darling'. Thanks so much for doing that."

He hesitated. "Oh, that's not necessary. It was my pleasure."

"No, please take it. It was my idea to buy the exact puzzle that the victim wanted. And as you pointed out," she sighed, "I seem to have a connection to it."

Jim took the money and slipped it into his pocket. "Thank you. What exactly do you intend to do with the puzzle?"

"I'll give Melinda Knight access to the box, in case she wants to test it for fingerprints or anything. You would have noticed that I got Mr. Blackstone to put it into the bag himself. Neither you nor I has touched it. It probably won't help the police much, but I'll offer it to her anyway."

"Good thinking," said Jim. "And what about the puzzle itself?"

"Oh, I'm planning to build that. It might be a fruitless exercise, but there must have been a reason why Paul

Robard was so determined to get that exact puzzle with those exact pieces. I'll put it together tonight and see if anything jumps out at me."

Jim laughed. "Tonight? It's a five-thousand-piece puzzle. It'll take you a lot more than one night. And puzzle-building works best as a group activity. If you try and do the whole thing on your own, your brain will get fried."

Luna rethought her strategy. It was obvious that she hadn't done any puzzle-building since those long-ago kindergarten days. "Maybe I'll put it out on the big table in the bookstore. That way we can all have a go at it."

"As long as no one tries to pinch any of the pieces."

"I'll set Pyewacket on them if they dare."

As they got to the bottom of Seagull Lane, they turned right onto Beach Road. To their left was the sea – a restless mass of gunmetal grey today. The wind snatched at Luna's long red hair as though it wanted to pluck it out. Ahead of them lay the famous Moonstone Island pier, home to a popular games arcade, several fast-food restaurants, and a casino, now under ownership by an Australian consortium. The wind carried the sound of mechanical bells and whistles to their ears. Even in the gloom, the pier was a cheerful sight, with its kaleidoscope of lights that flashed twenty-four hours a day.

Luna turned her attention to the path ahead. They were almost at Charmed now. Then she frowned and squinted as though she couldn't believe her eyes.

"Jim?" she ventured.

"Hmm?"

"Why is there a large chicken at the entrance to my bookstore?"

Chapter 6

*J*im followed the direction of her gaze. "That is no ordinary chicken – that's Sir Lancelot."

"Your sister's rooster?" The world tilted beneath Luna's feet. Sir Lancelot was a social media star whose exploits she followed on Instagram. He belonged at Kelvin Manor in Sussex – Jim's family estate that was run by his mother and sister – not at the entrance to Luna's bookstore.

"She must be visiting," said Jim. "That rooster goes everywhere with her. He even walks on a lead."

"Oh, I do hope Pyewacket isn't too cross about the unexpected guest."

But as Luna picked up the pace so that she was almost jogging towards the bookstore, her cat emerged from the doorway and very deliberately rubbed his head against the rooster's chunky body.

"Looks like you have nothing to worry about," said Jim.

"Thank goodness. I hate it when he's mad at me. He sulks."

As Jim reached the entrance of Charmed, he called for

his sister. "Bernadette, where are you? Show yourself. You've left your rooster on the pavement."

A tall woman with shoulder-length brown hair stood in the romance section with her nose buried deeply in a Victorian bodice-ripper. She looked up at this and turned around. Luna recognized her from Instagram. She and Jim were very similar in their facial features.

"Keep your hair on, little brother. Lancelot won't wander off once I've told him to stay put." She hugged Jim before holding him at arm's length and looking him up and down. "You look well, I must say. This island has always suited you."

"I didn't know you were coming to visit. Is Mum here too?"

"It was supposed to be a surprise. Should I have said, 'Surprise'? Probably, but I forgot. Yes, her ladyship is around here somewhere. I think she was meeting a friend for lunch."

"Viola," said Luna, suddenly putting it together. "She mentioned this morning that an old friend was coming to visit."

Bernadette glanced at her. "That's right. Mum and Viola go way back to their school days."

Jim gestured her forward. "Luna, I'd like you to meet my sister, Bernadette. Bernadette, this is Luna Larkspur."

"Bernie Cooke." She took Luna's hand in the firm clasp of a woman who worked with her hands. "This joker here is the only one who calls me Bernadette." She subjected Luna to the same critical look she had used on her brother. "You have the Larkspur look, if you don't mind my saying."

Luna pulled a face and flicked a strand of hair off her shoulder. "It's this red hair. It's a dead giveaway."

Bernie made a noise that sounded like 'pffft'. "Oh, come

off it. It's gorgeous, and you know it. Besides, why would you grow it so long if you didn't like it?"

Luna made a restless movement. "It doesn't like being cut."

She didn't know how else to put it. But it was true, and it was the reason why she still wore her hair cascading down her back like a five-year-old.

If Bernie found anything odd about this reply, she didn't say so.

"Hmm." She gave Luna a narrow look. "Well, anyway, it's good to meet you. I feel like I already know you from your Instagram."

Luna beamed. "I was just about to say that. I feel like I already know you from *your* Instagram. I definitely know Sir Lancelot over there."

"He's the cutest, isn't he? Although, I must say, that cat of yours comes a close second. Isn't it amazing how they've taken to each other?"

Luna looked at the doorway where the two animals sat side by side, leaning against each other like a couple of drunks outside a pub, propping each other up. They were attracting no little attention from the passersby.

"You should take photos for your Instagram," suggested Luna.

Bernie pulled her phone out of her skirt pocket. "You're right! This is A-plus content."

But before she could paparazzi the bird and cat, Jim pounced on her left hand. "Hey, what's this?" He tapped the pretty white-gold band with a small, brilliant-cut diamond on it.

"Oh, that." Bernie's cheeks pinkened. "I was about to say. Congratulate me, little brother. I'm getting married."

Jim's eyes widened. "You and Diana finally got engaged?"

"What? No, not Diana. We broke up weeks ago. Didn't I tell you? No, this is Flora."

Jim rocked back on his heels. "Wait, *what*? You broke *up*? And a few weeks later you're engaged to someone else?"

Bernie shrugged. "When it's right, it's right."

"But you and Diana were together for – what? – six years?"

"Which just goes to show that she wasn't Ms. Right. No one waits six years to move the relationship forward unless you have some serious doubts. We both knew it wasn't forever. We decided to let each other go so we could find happiness separately."

Jim opened and closed his mouth like a goldfish. "But, still ... I mean ... to get engaged after just a few weeks. Please tell me you're having a long engagement."

Bernie's smile was cheerful. "Not at all. Flora is sending out save-the-date cards as we speak. It will be a winter wonderland wedding, just before Christmas. Are you ready to be best man, Jimmy?"

Jim still looked shell-shocked. "Of course. It would be my honor. But ... but ..."

"This is where you congratulate me, little brother."

He caught her in a hard hug. "Of course, I do. I congratulate you with all of my heart. I will keep reminding myself that you are a strong, independent woman who knows her own mind."

Bernie patted his shoulder. "There you go. That's better." She turned to Luna. "I need to dash to the covered market to do some shopping. Is it all right if I leave Sir Lancelot here while I'm gone? I'll pop him into his run now so he can eat and drink and have a bit of a snooze."

She indicated an open cage, about three feet long, that had been set up as a kind of luxury hotel for chickens.

There was food and water and plenty of straw for him to root around in.

"Of course," said Luna. "He's my cat's best friend now. He is welcome any time."

"Thanks. I won't be long." Bernie popped Sir Lancelot into his run, where he pecked contentedly among the straw. Then she scooped up her bag and headed out towards the covered market.

∿

Jim blew out a breath when she was gone and shook his head. "A strong, independent woman," he reminded himself. "A strong, independent woman." He lifted the shopping bag he was still carrying and swung it from side to side. "Where do you want this?"

Luna looked around the store. It was so big, with so many rooms that led into each other, that there was sure to be a suitable table somewhere. She walked into the nonfiction section and tapped a large, rectangular table that was currently supporting her Recent Releases display.

"How about this? I'll move this display onto the smaller, oval table. Will this be big enough?"

Jim slid the box out of the shopping bag and examined it. "It says here the puzzle will measure one by one and a half meters when it is made up. That table should be fine."

Luna tried to remember what a meter was. A couple of feet, maybe?

Still taking care not to touch the box, Jim deposited it on the table.

"Thanks," said Luna. "And thanks for carrying it all the way from the Scout Hall. You probably need to get on with your work now. This is a late start for you."

"Yes, indeed. Duty calls." Jim brought a coffee and a cookie from Harper before settling himself in the permanent collection with his laptop open.

Luna gave the puzzle box a suspicious glance. She hadn't forgiven it for glowing in such a conspicuous fashion, and nor did she trust it not to do so again. Determined to be practical, she marched to the little kitchen she had set up next to the coffee hatch and pulled on a pair of thick rubber gloves. They were bright pink, and she felt silly wearing them, but they should do the trick.

Back at the table, she put off the moment of truth by moving the Recent Releases display to its new home on the oval table. Then she took a deep breath and picked up the puzzle box in both gloved hands. It immediately started glowing again, so brightly that she could hardly bear to look at it.

"Darn it!" She dropped the box like it was hot and watched the glow fade away to nothing.

Harper came hurrying over. "That was so cool. Do it again."

Luna gave her a grumpy look. "It's not cool – it's annoying. This is a piece of evidence. I need to open it without attracting too much attention." She pulled off the gloves and pushed them towards Harper. "You do it."

"Sure, but why do I need the gloves? *I'm* not a human glow stick."

"I'm trying not to get fingerprints on the box. I'm saving it for D.S. Knight and her team."

Harper fetched a letter opener from Luna's desk and used it to pierce the plastic wrapping around the box. "Why does this thing look secondhand?"

"Because it is. It's definitely not new. That's why I only

paid two hundred and eighty pounds for it, instead of three hundred."

Harper's eyes looked like they wanted to pop out of their sockets. "Two hundred and eighty pounds? For a *jigsaw puzzle*? You were robbed."

"It's supposed to be some fancy, vintage, hand-made puzzle, but yes, I agree that I was robbed."

"What's so special about it anyway? Why did you want it?"

"It was the last thing Paul Robard tried to buy before he was killed. He was desperate to own this specific puzzle, but didn't have enough money. I want to find out why he wanted it so badly."

Harper opened the box and tipped the puzzle pieces slowly onto the table. "That's interesting. Are you going to try and build it? It'll take ages. But I'll help." Her gloved fingers reached automatically for a corner piece.

"Please do. I was just telling Jim I haven't done one of these since I left kindergarten." Luna fingered one of the pieces. Then she dropped it when it started to glow. "Oh, for goodness' sake. Not the puzzle pieces too."

Harper suppressed her grin when she saw how annoyed Luna was. "Can't you do something to stop that from happening?"

"Like what? Even rubber gloves don't help."

I meant something more like ... like ..."

"Like what?"

"Like a ..." Harper lowered her voice. "Like a *spell* or something."

Luna sighed. "That's the problem. I don't know any."

They looked up as the door chime sounded.

"There you go," said Harper. "There's someone who can help you."

Chapter 7

*L*una stared at the vision in purple that had entered the bookstore.

The vision wore a loose purple house dress with black gumboots and what could only be described as a cloak. She had long, grey, frizzy hair and silver rings on every finger. Her habitual expression was pleasant, but right now she looked cranky.

"Gosh," said Luna. "It's Matilda Bobbit."

Harper walked forward. "Matilda! You're in town. There'll be pigs flying overhead next."

Matilda bent a critical eye on her. "You're a Brave, aren't you?"

"Yes, I am. Harper Brave, at your service."

"Hmm. One of the hardware-store Braves?"

"No. We're the Kwikmart Braves."

"Matilda thought for a moment. "So, it's probably your brother who delivers my groceries, right?"

"On the scooter? Yes, that's my brother, Pete. He's not all that keen on your dogs."

Matilda made a humphing sound. "Stuff and nonsense. I tie them up when I know he's coming. Mostly."

Harper cocked her head. "What brings you into the village, Matilda? It's been months."

"Actually, I wanted to speak to this one." She jerked her thumb in Luna's direction.

"Okay," said Harper. "I'll leave you to it then." She retired to the coffee station where Luna could almost see her ears flapping in an effort to keep tabs on their conversation.

"Can I get you a coffee?" asked Luna. "The first one is on the house."

"I won't say no then. A cappuccino, please."

Harper brought it over and Matilda took the first sip and closed her eyes.

"Oh, that's good. That's so good it might lure me down into the village more frequently in future. I don't suppose you deliver up Munro Drive?"

"I'm afraid we don't deliver at all, although that's something we could think about in the future." Luna watched Matilda drink her coffee and thought of all the things she should be doing with her morning. "Was there something you wanted to see me about?"

"As a matter of fact," said Matilda, her voice gruff. "I wanted to thank you for the scarf you gave me. I know it belonged to your great-great-grandmother. There's a photo of her wearing it. I just wanted you to know ... it means a lot to me."

"I see you're wearing it today."

Matilda touched the purple silk. "I wear it every day."

Luna smiled. It was only a few weeks earlier that she had made the pilgrimage up Munro Drive to one of the most remote parts of the island. She had wanted to visit

Matilda Bobbit who had a reputation for being a white witch. Luna had quickly sensed a lack of power in her, but had to admit that Matilda understood the craft and discipline of magic in a way that Luna didn't. Plus, the three giant Siberian huskies that so terrified Pete Brave were absolute darlings. Luna had fallen in love with them at first sight.

"Actually." Matilda frowned. "I'm not entirely sure why I felt compelled to come into the village today. Saying thanks to you doesn't seem like a good enough reason, if you don't mind my saying. And I haven't any shopping to do. It's a bit of a mystery."

Luna knew then that it was her own hunger for Matilda's guidance that had pulled her down from her hermit life up on the hill. But she wasn't about to tell her that.

"It's a mystery," she agreed. "But since you're here anyway, I wonder if you could help me with something?"

Matilda finished her coffee and put down the cup. "Shoot."

Luna beckoned her to the non-fiction section where the puzzle still laid spilled out on the table.

"Watch this." She picked up one of the puzzle pieces and held it out towards Matilda. As it began to glow like a small sun, Matilda's mouth fell open and she staggered back a full step. "That's some kind of a trick, isn't it? It's a child's toy. It must be."

Luna put the piece back on the table and watched as the glow faded.

Fascinated, Matilda picked up the same piece and turned it around in her hand, looking for the button or switch. When it became clear that there wasn't one, she put it down and swallowed hard.

"What exactly is the problem here?"

Luna waved her hands in frustration. "I want to build

this puzzle. I need to be able to handle these pieces without glowing like a searchlight. And I want to be able to work on the puzzle here in full view of everyone, without attracting attention. I even tried wearing rubber gloves. Nothing helps."

"Do it again," said Matilda, indicating the puzzle pieces. "With a different piece this time."

With a sigh, Luna scooped up a handful of the puzzle pieces. They began to glow with an almost painful intensity.

Matilda shaded her eyes. "Okay, put them down. I get it."

"You see my problem?"

Matilda paced in a tight circle, thinking hard. She came to a halt in front of Luna. "I would have thought that a simple blocking charm would suffice, but I presume you've tried that already."

Luna looked down at her hands. "Um ... I haven't actually. You see the problem is - I don't really know how to do that."

Matilda scoffed. "What do you mean you don't know how? What kind of a witch do you call yourself anyway?"

"I don't call myself a ... what you said ... at all. I told you I knew nothing. I told you I was a rank beginner. This is why I need your help."

Matilda tutted. "Your great-great-grandmother must be rolling in her grave. Why, even I know how to do a simple blocking charm. I use them to keep people away from my farm. It works like a ... well, like a charm."

Luna suspected that Porky, Bugs and Daffy – Matilda's three horse-sized dogs had more to do with keeping people off her farm than any blocking charm she might have come up with. But she needed to know more. "Tell me about these blocking charms."

"Nothing could be easier. You use your standard

blocking ingredients – your rubber, your cork, your rosemary and rue. Then bing, bang, boom, you're done."

"I'm not too sure about that middle part. The bing, bang,
boom part."

Matilda made a sweeping gesture that encompassed the
whole bookstore. "You must surely have a book of instructions somewhere amongst this lot. Coco certainly did."

Luna held up a finger. "Wait here." Then she trotted
upstairs to her apartment to grab the Larkspur Family
Recipe book. She paged through it as she came downstairs,
hoping that something would catch her eye.

"This looks promising." Hovering on the bottom step,
she read through it.

Ingredients

    1 scant ounce of rubber-infused bark
    1 scant ounce of cork-infused bark
    3 sprigs of fresh rosemary
    4 leaves of dried rue
    8 fluid ounces of enchanted water
    Sugar to taste

Method

    *When harvesting your rubber and cork, remember the gener-
ations of Larkspurs that will come after you. It is not necessary to
cut down a tree to access the properties you need. Those were the
wasteful habits of our ancestors, and they need to cease immediately. There is sufficient rubber and cork in the bark of these
respective trees that one does not need to violate their cores. Be a
responsible person and leave this resource intact for future
generations.*

Boil your ounce of rubber briskly in two fluid ounces of enchanted water for ten minutes to extract the rubber.

Add a further fluid ounce of enchanted water to the mixture and remove the bark of the rubber tree. Add the bark of the cork tree and boil briskly for a further ten minutes.

Extract the cork bark and throw away.

Add the remaining five fluid ounces of enchanted water as well as the rosemary and rue.

Bring to a rolling boil for fifteen minutes.

Strain well.

Allow to cool completely.

Drink with sugar added to taste (this mixture is extremely bitter. You will find it unpalatable without sugar).

This recipe will supply two doses. Store in a cool place for up to five days.

This preparation provides an efficacious shield against power. Whether you are trying to keep power in or out, this will be effective for up to two days.

"What do you think of this?" Luna wandered into the nonfiction section where Matilda waited. She put the book in front of her, open at the correct page.

"*A simple shielding charm to keep power in or out,*" Matilda read. "This looks like the business." She tapped the recipe. "And look, it contains all the ingredients I said."

"You were right."

Curious, Matilda paged through the book. "What was that recipe doing in the middle of this blank book? It seems a funny place to find it."

"It's not ..." Luna looked more closely at Matilda's face. Her eyes were blank and unfocused as she paged through the recipe book. Only when she came to the shielding charm did her eyes focus and seem to see the words on the page.

Luna knew this wasn't something she was doing. Somehow – as crazy as it sounded – the book was doing it. It would only allow Matilda to see the specific recipe Luna was showing her.

She shrugged and changed tack. "I know. It's weird, isn't it? My late grandfather had several books like that."

Matilda muttered to herself as she read over the recipe. "Enchanted water ... never had much luck with that myself, although I have a good recipe for it. I suppose it will be different for you. You won't mind if I just ..." She pulled out her phone and snapped a picture of the recipe.

Luna's heart jumped for a second, but she decided not to protest. Matilda was being very generous with her advice, after all. Besides, Luna strongly suspected that the photograph would be blank when Matilda came to look at it later on. And even if it weren't, Matilda's fundamental inability to make enchanted water would render the recipe ineffectual.

Matilda looked up from the recipe book and frowned. "I've been meaning to ask – why have you turned your bookstore into some kind of barnyard?"

Luna saw she was glaring at the chicken coop which currently housed Sir Lancelot, who appeared to be asleep with his beak resting on his feathery chest, and Pyewacket who had hopped into the coop and was sprawled out next to his new best friend.

"Oh, he belongs to a friend. She'll be back to pick him up soon."

Matilda gave a disapproving sniff. "Well, at any rate, you be sure not to drink this charm like it says there in the recipe, see?"

Chapter 8

"Wait a minute," said Luna as Matilda prepared to leave. "What do you mean I mustn't drink it? What else would I do with it?"

Matilda slung her bag over her shoulder. "Always think through the possible consequences of a charm before using it. Imagine yourself drinking a full dose of that blocking charm. Would it only block your power from leaking out through your fingertips?"

Luna thought about this. "No. It would block my power completely, wouldn't it?"

"For a couple of days, yes. You have to ask yourself whether now is a good time for that – for you to be effectively powerless."

Luna thought about the next few days and how she had planned to busy herself with the investigation into the death of Paul Robard.

"No," she said. "This is not a good time for it at all. But what can I do? I need to build this puzzle."

Matilda tapped a forefinger against her temple. "Think outside the box, girl. Coco was particularly good at that. Mix it in with your hand cream, for heaven's sake. You'll have to experiment to get the right strength, but you'll get there eventually."

With the air of one who is done with people for the day, Matilda marched out of the bookstore, pausing only for a last tut at the chicken coop.

Luna poured herself a much-needed glass of cold water and sank into her chair behind her desk. Once again, Matilda had made her feel like a clueless beginner. Which, in all fairness, was what she was. But she wasn't used to being made to feel quite so incompetent.

At least some people on this island still respected her.

The first person who came to mind was Melinda Knight. It was high time that Luna sent her an update. She messaged her.

I've just bought the jigsaw puzzle that Paul Robard was supposedly interested in minutes before his death. He insisted on having this specific five-thousand-piece puzzle, even though he couldn't afford it.

Melinda's reply came quickly.

Five THOUSAND pieces?? Who has that kind of time?

Luna smiled.

I'm going to build it to see if I can figure out why he was so interested in these particular puzzle pieces. I've saved the box and the plastic it was wrapped in if you want to dust it for fingerprints. The only other person who handled it was the seller.

There was a pause as Melinda seemed to think about this.

Okay, I'll send someone to see if we can lift any fingerprints off the box or plastic.

Luna tapped out a reply.

You might want to re-interview a Mr. Blackstone who runs the Architectural Interest stand in the scout hall. He had quite an argument with Robard before he died.

Melissa replied quickly.

I'll do that, thanks.

"I'm heading out to lunch now, boss." Harper skipped past Luna's desk. "I need some sea air to clear my head."

"Enjoy." Luna went to sit at the serving hatch next to the coffee machine. She took her laptop with her as she planned to find out what sort of digital footprint Paul Robard had left behind him.

"Who were you exactly, Mr. Robard?" she muttered as she began to Google his name.

'Paul Robard' brought up too many results to be useful. Searching 'Paul Robard Yorkshire' narrowed it down considerably. Two different people showed up in the results, but Luna found a photograph confirming that Paul Matthew Robard was the man she was looking for.

It seemed that he had been a kind of professional hobbyist. He had owned a hobby store in Leeds, one of the bigger cities in Yorkshire. He had a Linked In page on which he described himself as a life-long hobby enthusiast. He didn't have a personal Facebook profile, but his hobby shop had its own Facebook page. This suggested that his store had recently begun offering its merchandise for sale online as well as from their physical premises in Leeds.

More digging revealed that the shop had recently downsized. It now occupied a third of its previous floor space. Robard's Hobbies now had a branded sneaker store as its neighbor. This struck Luna as an obvious cost-cutting measure. If Robard had owned the premises, he would have generated capital by selling two-thirds of it off to the sneaker store. If he only rented the premises, this would have cut his monthly rent by up to two-thirds.

Browsing through the store's catalogue on the website, Luna saw that jigsaw puzzles made up a significant part of their stock. It seemed logical to assume that his visit to Moonstone Island for the jigsaw puzzle convention was a business trip, rather than a personal one. It shed no light on what could have caused his death.

Going further back in time, Luna discovered an interview that he had given to a hobby magazine ten years' earlier. His shop had been at the peak of its success then.

My hobbies got me through difficult time, says Paul Robard.

Paul Robard of Robard's Hobbies is a well-known figure in the hobby community. His sprawling store in central Leeds is a treasure trove for enthusiasts. He specializes in hard-to-find stock and in being able to source almost any item for a customer, even if it is on the other side of the world.

You won't find the usual brand names at Robard's Hobbies. He seeks out little-known hand-crafted, and vintage items that will appeal to every collector's heart.

I interviewed Paul Robard for this article and asked how he came to pursue a career in hobbies.

"I didn't have an easy time of it growing up," said Mr. Robard. "Hobbies were my solace and my escape."

I asked Mr. Robard if he could remember the first hobby he fell in love with as a child and he told me that it was a secondhand plastic yoyo that a foster parent gave him. "I lived in foster care for a while before I was adopted by the people who are my family now. I don't have many happy memories from that time, but I do remember one foster parent giving me an old yoyo to play with. He also gave me an instruction sheet with diagrams showing how to do tricks with the yoyo, like 'walk the dog' and 'rock the cradle'. I was instantly hooked and spent every waking moment practicing my tricks."

Mr. Robard's interests expanded to board games, jigsaw puzzles, Rubik's cubes, and action figures. He started working in the now defunct Blackstone's Hobby Store at the age of sixteen. By eighteen, he began appearing at flea markets to sell some of his excess stock. This was so successful that just a few years later he was able to open Robard's Hobbies, which then expanded into the store that is so beloved among the hobby community today.

Two pieces of information caught Luna's attention in the article. The first was that Paul Robard had spent time in the foster care system as a young boy. This didn't gel with the information that his sister Tina had given her, which was that he had been adopted at birth. It seemed as though the parents that were now his adoptive family had come into his life at a later stage. Luna wanted to find out more about that.

Then there was the snippet of information that Robard had worked at a place called Blackstone's Hobby Shop as a teenager. It wasn't a common name, and Luna believed it would be worth finding out whether that Blackstone was connected in any way to the person Paul Robard had spoken to just before his death. If there was a connection – if it were possibly even the same man – then he had lied to Luna and Jim about not knowing Robard before they met at the puzzle convention.

Luna kept searching, going deeper into the unfrequented corners of the internet. She found a hobbyists' chat room where a user by the name of Puzzlemeister Robard had been active in recent months. Some of the posts were publicly visible, but others were hidden – available only to approved members of the chat room. In a reply to one of the public posts, another user addressed Puzzlemeister Robard as Paul. Luna was sure she was on the right track.

She went through the process of signing up to the chat room and received an automated reply saying that her application was under consideration and that a moderator would reply soon.

Luna was just wondering what constituted 'soon' when a sudden crowing noise startled her. Sir Lancelot had woken up from his nap, apparently thinking that it was morning. Luna had heard roosters before, but never indoors, or at such close range. The sound was quite deafening.

"Loud, isn't he?" Jim appeared next to her with a fork in one hand and a container full of chicken salad in the other. It wasn't unusual for him to sit with her while he ate his lunch. Luna didn't mind. She found it companionable.

"I'd better eat too," she said. "When Harper comes back, I plan to spend my lunch hour upstairs working on a recipe that Matilda suggested."

Jim shook his head. "You really think she can be helpful to you?"

"Oh, definitely. She gave me some excellent advice. Soon I'll be able to handle those puzzle pieces without lighting up the room like a Roman candle. I just need to pop to the covered market to get some rue."

"Rue? Now there's a Shakespearean herb. I wonder if you'll be able to find it."

"Ellie Granger will have it."

"You're probably right. Speaking of the puzzle pieces - I did some of the puzzle for you. The frame is in place and a bit of the bottom right corner. No revelations have come to light yet. It looks like it does on the box – a high street scene from the 1920s."

Luna went to see for herself. Jim was right. So far, the developing puzzle looked exactly like it did on the box.

"Thanks for doing that." She slid back into her seat and took out the sandwich she had prepared for lunch. "Any time you feel like working on it, please go ahead. I'll tell Harper the same. In fact, maybe I should throw it open to the public. Any Charmed customer who wants to work on the puzzle can do so."

Jim looked dubious. "What if someone took a puzzle piece? Or damaged one?"

"Pyewacket would bite them on the ankle. He's a really good guard cat."

Jim laughed. "Then go ahead. The security in this place is tight."

Luna munched on her sandwich, thinking about everything she had learnt that morning. "I Googled Paul Robard earlier," she told Jim. "Apparently, he worked at a store called Blackstone's Hobbies in Leeds as a teenager. Do you think that's the same Mr. Blackstone we spoke to? Because if it is, he must have been lying about never having seen Paul before."

"Not necessarily. The owner of a shop doesn't always remember his employees. If he owned the shop but seldom went in there, it's quite possible that he wouldn't remember a teenager who worked there years ago."

"That's true."

Jim looked up as the door chime sounded. "Isn't that one of D.S. Knight's team?"

"Yes. He's going to dust the puzzle box for fingerprints."

"And there's the Detective Sergeant herself coming in after him."

Chapter 9

$\mathcal{L}$una showed the scene-of-crime officer the box that the jigsaw puzzle had been in and the plastic that had been used to wrap it. He set about daubing both with fingerprint powder.

When she returned to the coffee station, Melinda had pulled up a chair next to Jim. It seemed she had settled in for a chat.

"Coffee?" offered Luna. "Cookie?"

"Yes, to both. I had one of those cookies at book club last night, so I know how good they are."

"I found out something interesting about Paul Robard," Luna said as she set about filling Melinda's order. "It was in an article he wrote for a hobby magazine. He said that he had been in foster care as a young boy and only adopted later. His sister Tina made it sound as though he was adopted at birth."

Melinda bit into her cookie. "That's right. We accessed his records this morning. It's a sad story. Apparently, the first adoption didn't work out. The couple that adopted him found him too disruptive. He went into the foster care system for a few years until one of the families that was fostering him wanted to adopt him. It was a very happy arrangement, I believe."

Luna stared at her. "Wait a minute. Hold up. You mean his original adoptive family just returned him, like taking a puppy back to the pound?"

"Well, not exactly like that, but essentially, yes."

"You can do that? Return a child? Surely once you've adopted a baby, you have a legal obligation to it?"

"The courts take into account what is in the best interests of the child. And being raised by reluctant parents is generally not it. Even biological parents can put their children into the foster care system. I told you it was a sad story. He was just four when his first family gave him up."

Melinda swallowed hard. Luna knew she was thinking about her own son who would be four at his next birthday.

"That must have been a rough start in life," said Jim. "First his biological parents didn't want him and then his adoptive parents didn't want him either. That's got to have an effect on you."

"It's no wonder he turned to hobbies for comfort," said Luna. "By the way, did you know that the first hobby shop he worked in as a teenager was owned by the man who sold me that jigsaw puzzle? Or at least, it's the same surname."

Melinda made a note on her note pad. "Blackstone, right? No, I didn't know that. There might be a history there. Oh, you should probably be aware that members of both his biological family and adoptive families are due to arrive on the island soon. And since most people tend to wash up here at Charmed sooner or later, I wanted to give you advance warning."

"Okay. I mean, they probably won't, but that's good to know."

Melinda finished her coffee and stood up. Her scene-of-crime officer was ready to go.

"Did you get anything?" she asked him.

"Three full prints and six partials, ma'am. I'll run them through the data base back at the station. Oh, and I cleaned up as best I could."

"Thank you, Mellis." Melinda turned to Luna. "You can throw away the plastic, but I presume you'll be keeping the box. Let me know if anything interesting emerges when you build that puzzle." She said goodbye to Luna and Jim and left with her officer in tow.

～

Harper returned from her lunch break promptly at one o'clock. Luna excused herself to go upstairs.

But first she took a piece of poster board and a Sharpie out of her desk. She folded the board in half and wrote on both halves, *Please help us to build this puzzle. If you remove or damage any pieces, the cat will bite your ankle.*

She added a cartoon drawing of a toothy cat for good measure. Then she propped it up like a place card next to the jigsaw puzzle.

Her final step was to wake Pyewacket up from the nap he was enjoying next to his new best friend, Sir Lancelot. She accomplished this by stroking him from head to tail. He responded by making what she always thought of as his activation noise, which sounded like *Mrrow?*

Luna bent down and whispered in his ear, "Guard the jigsaw puzzle."

She had no doubt that he would understand her. He was an intelligent animal.

Pyewacket stretched luxuriously and hopped out of the

coop. Only once he had washed himself all over, did he take up his post next to the jigsaw puzzle table.

Luna was about to go upstairs when Sir Lancelot woke up too. He pecked around the chicken coop for bits of grain and corn before fluttering out and taking up his position at the cat's side.

The two of them were too restless after their nap to sit still for long. They began wrestling and play-fighting. Luna was pleased that she had the presence of mind to take out her phone and capture some of it on video. She would send it to Jim's sister to use on her Instagram account. Then she caught sight of the time and saw that she had only forty-five minutes of her lunch break left. She galloped out the door to buy some rue.

Few things made Luna feel more like a beginner than struggling her way through a new recipe for a charm. It wasn't like baking. That always made her feel competent in the kitchen. This made her feel like the rawest of rookies.

She decided to start with the enchanted water this time. Charm recipes always assumed you had it ready. The problem with enchanted water was that you couldn't make it in advance and store it. You had to use it immediately and discard any excess.

She went through the motions of preparing it. It still made her blush to remember the last incantation she had used, which was *bippity boppity boo*. She had lifted it straight from her childhood memories of Disney movies.

At least this time she had come up with something new – an incantation that had the advantage of originality, if nothing else.

Using the same piece of elm she had employed last time, she twirled the point around the shallow bowl of water and said, "Water light, water bright, share with me your hidden might."

Okay, it wasn't Wordsworth, but it would do the trick until she came up with something different.

The water stirred restlessly for a moment before settling down and acquiring a kind of shimmer. Last time Luna had thought she was imagining that sheen on the surface. Now she recognized it for what it was – a sign that the preparation had worked.

She lined up her other ingredients. There was the fresh and dried rosemary from her own supplies, and the fresh and dried rue from Ellie Granger's shop in the covered market. She heated them slowly in the enchanted water, resisting the urge to try to hurry the process. Experience had taught her that the 'allow to stand' and 'allow to cool' instructions were a vital part of the preparation of charms. Skipping or accelerating those parts of the recipe would yield an inferior result.

She strained the final product into a glass jar and covered it. It should be completely cool by the end of the working day, at which time Luna could begin experimenting with mixing it into a hand cream.

～

Luna got downstairs to discover both rooster and mobile chicken coop missing.

"Was your sister here?" she asked Jim.

"Yes. She and my mother are spending the night on the island. That wasn't the original plan, but now that they've got started on wedding shopping, they can't tear themselves away."

Luna would have thought that a major urban center –

like London, for example – would have been more suitable for wedding shopping. But Moonstone Island certainly offered a unique retail experience.

"Have they checked into a hotel?"

"They're staying at the same B&B I always use when I'm here. Oh, I nearly forgot." He slapped himself on the forehead. "You're invited to dinner."

"I'm invited to dinner?"

"Yes, tonight. My mother wants to meet you."

"Me? Are you sure?"

Jim broke eye contact and stared at the floor. "Yes. I guess she ... uh ... heard about the budding friendship between Sir Lancelot and Pyewacket. She wants to make sure that her grand-rooster's new best friend comes from a good family."

Luna laughed. "Of course she does. Well, I'm very happy to accept. Where and what time?"

"Seven pm at the Grand Hotel. My mother always dines there when she's in town."

Luna swallowed. "The Grand Hotel. Right. Yes, absolutely."

She would have preferred almost anywhere else. The Grand Hotel was both stuffy and prim. In this informal beachside village, where candy apples and fish 'n chips eaten out the bag with your fingers were the order of the day, the Grand seemed to belong to a different century.

The choice of venue made her even more nervous about meeting Jim's mother. Luna had done a little light stalking of Jim's mother already, via the internet. The dowager Lady Kelvin popped up on Bernie's Instagram page from time to time and featured in news reports of charity functions and aristocratic get-togethers. While Jim favored the British academic look, like Hugh Grant in *Notting Hill,* and Bernie dressed like a sensible lady farmer, their mother was a different creature altogether. Her regular uniform seemed to be a twinset and pearls worn with a tweed skirt, pantyhose, and court shoes. Her hair was always perfectly coiffed and her makeup immaculate. She looked – in the most alarming way possible – rather like the late queen.

Just looking at photographs of her made Luna feel very American and even more self-conscious. She felt as though she had something to prove. She felt obliged to demonstrate that she had not been raised in a barn.

With the prospect of a stressful evening ahead, Luna decided to make the best possible use of the afternoon. This involved tackling a task she had been avoiding for weeks, namely unpacking the boxes of merchandise she had ordered.

Harper had recently told her that the customers were asking for gift and novelty items like bookmarks, pens, and diaries. She had expressed the opinion that Luna was leaving money on the table by not stocking these and other non-book items. So Luna had gone through a supplier's catalogue and ordered a whole lot of what she liked to think of as book-adjacent products that she wanted to offer in her store.

These items had arrived as scheduled, but she hadn't got around to unpacking them yet. As the days turned into weeks and the boxes still languished behind her desk, she decided that this was getting ridiculous. It was time to make a start.

It wasn't as though she was betraying her grandfather's principles by selling items that weren't strictly speaking books. Red Ricky Larkspur had paid precious little attention to the running of the shop, preferring to devote himself to betting on horseracing. He would not be in the slightest bit disappointed with Luna for giving up some of her floor space to non-book items. On the contrary, he would probably admire her hustle.

It was time to get over herself and make a start.

As she cut open the first box, she couldn't help being delighted by what she saw. It was a collection of globes of all different sizes, highlighting different aspects of the world. One of the most fun was a globe that showed the hometowns of a hundred different authors throughout history.

Luna settled down to unpacking them with a sense that this might not be so bad after all.

Chapter 10

"Can I help?" asked Harper. "The coffee station is quiet at the moment. We always have a lull after lunch."

Luna looked at the boxes she had broken open. "Could you set up a point-of-sale display by the cash register? Choose some of the smaller items that people would be more likely to buy on impulse. Something they can stare at while they're standing in line waiting to be served." She caught Harper's eye and laughed. "Okay, we don't often get actual lines forming at the cash register, but it could happen."

"Optimistic thinking. I like it." Harper joined Luna in staring at the merchandise. "So, I'm thinking the 3D bookmarks need to go by the till, along with these little clip-on book lights for reading in bed at night, and maybe those cute pencils with the novelty erasers on the back. Oh, and these wee inspirational desk calendars with a different motivational message for each day."

Luna nodded. "Perfect. You have good instincts."

"What about at the coffee station? Should we display any of these items over there?"

"Let's put that idea on the back burner for now. The coffee station is doing great business and I want people focused on caffeine and cookies when they're in line there."

Harper sighed. "They're already thinking about your cookies. All you need to do is make more of them. Forty-eight is not enough. You put out twenty-four in the morning, and I put out twenty-four after lunch, and they disappear very quickly. You could make double that amount – even triple – and they would all sell."

Luna pulled a face. "I just can't seem to get enthusiastic about spending even more time baking every evening. At the moment it's fine. I can keep this up six days a week, no problem. But doubling or tripling my output would just be onerous. You know how tiny my kitchen is."

"Then maybe it's time to look into getting an outside supplier."

"Store-bought?" Luna pulled a face. "The customers will know the difference and they won't be happy about it."

"I wasn't thinking of store bought, exactly. There are a number of people on the island who make baked goods in their own homes for sale at different outlets in the village. Obviously, some are better than others, but still, the standard is pretty high. I'm not saying they could compete with your magical cookies, but they're still delicious."

Luna made a huffing sound. "My cookies aren't magical. They're just regular. I don't *do* anything to them."

"You don't have to. They just are exceptional."

"An outside supplier," Luna mused. "Is there anyone in particular you could recommend?"

"I can think of three or four off the top of my head. I'll

write them down for you. And then of course there's my aunt, but I don't want to put her forward."

"Your aunt? Not the estate agent?"

"No, different aunt."

"One of the Kwikmart Braves?"

"One of the hardware-store Braves. But, like I say, I don't want to put her forward. We should have, like, a blind tasting or something."

"Ooh, fun!" Luna liked the sound of that.

"We could get Jim in on it too. He's a cookie fan."

Pleased with her idea, Harper took a box of merchandise to the cash register where she began to unpack it and display it in the clear Perspex stands and holders Luna had ordered.

Luna finished unpacking the globes and moved on to the diaries and Moleskine notebooks. As she moved onto the jigsaw puzzles, the association made her glance into the non-fiction section where she had set up the mysterious puzzle. A small man wearing a newsboy cap and blue jeans with braces over a checked shirt was working on it. Pyewacket sat on the table next to him. His paws were folded under his chest in a relaxed attitude, but his blue eyes followed every move the man made. He was on guard.

Luna finished arranging the puzzle boxes before taking a casual stroll to the non-fiction section. She wasn't sure what drew her to talk to the man, except that he seemed to have provoked a suspicious attitude in her cat.

"Hello." She gave him a friendly smile. "I'm Luna. How are you getting on with the puzzle?" She glanced down and saw that he had added at least a couple of hundred pieces in the time that he had been busy. "Oh, wow. You've made great progress."

"Thank you." He met her eyes briefly before turning his

attention to the unplaced pieces. He scanned them slowly until he found the piece he was looking for. Pinching it between finger and thumb, he held it up to the light. "This is a remarkable puzzle. Hand-tooled and hand-crafted. And every piece fits seamlessly. It's a work of art."

"So I'm told. I bought it because it represents a period in the island's history that I happen to be very interested in. Moonstone Village in the nineteen-twenties. I plan to frame it when it's done."

The man clicked his tongue. "The nineteen-twenties? No, this dates from the nineteen-thirties. The late nineteen-thirties, I would say."

Luna leaned in for a closer look. "How can you tell?"

"Do you see that patriotic red and blue bunting that some of the shopfronts are displaying? It's quite a distinctive design. I'm not a historian, but I do know how to date jigsaw puzzles. That bunting was hung by certain business owners on the island as an expression of patriotism shortly after war was declared in 1938. I could be wrong of course, but I don't think I am."

Luna frowned at the little blue and red flags that were starting to appear as the puzzle progressed. She noticed something.

"That's odd. The picture on the box doesn't include the bunting."

"That's right. The picture on the box and the puzzle inside don't match. The box shows a street scene from the nineteen-twenties, while the puzzle shows the same street scene from the late nineteen-thirties. They must have been mismatched at some point. It's all rather intriguing."

"I guess you're in town for the jigsaw puzzle convention?" Luna asked.

"Correct. Peter Pipstow at your service." He shook hands

with Luna. "I sell hobby items via my website. We stock several vintage jigsaw puzzles. But don't worry – I won't try to pinch this one. This chap is keeping a close eye on me." He indicated Pyewacket.

"He's a terror, all right," said Luna. "So, you don't have a brick-and-mortar store? You sell over the internet?"

"It's all virtual, except for the actual games and hobbies themselves," said Peter. "Those are tangible. The overheads of running a physical storefront are just unaffordable. Yes, you miss out on foot traffic and casual browsers, but most hobbyists hang out online anyway. I know where to reach them." He gestured around the shop. "You probably know all this, working in a place like Charmed."

"It's an old family business. There's no rental or mortgage to pay. That makes a big difference."

"I imagine it would. The internet has been good to me, but I remain nostalgic for the old days. I used to work in a hobby shop when I was younger."

Luna pricked up her ears. "Is that so? Which one?"

"The great Blackstone's Hobby Shop in Leeds."

"Oh, I've heard of it. It was a Mr. Blackstone who sold me this puzzle at the convention this morning. Was he the owner?"

"He was indeed. I often see him at hobby-related events. He had to give up the store in the end. Now he operates mostly online like I do, but also out of the garage of his house."

Luna scanned Peter's face, judging him to be approximately the same age as Paul Robard. "How old were you when you worked in his shop?"

"I was a kid. It was my first job. I think I started there when I was sixteen or seventeen."

"Does Blackstone remember you from that time?"

"I think he does. He has certainly got to know me in recent years now that we're in the same line of work. And he knows I used to work for him. I can't say for sure whether he specifically remembers me from when I was a teenager. Why do you ask?"

"I was thinking that you must have known the man who was killed at the convention last night. He used to work at Blackstone's too."

"You mean Paul Robard? Of course I knew him. He was an integral part of the games and hobby community. We worked together at Blackstone's back in the day. It's such an awful thing that happened to him. We are still reeling."

"Did you see him at all yesterday?

"Briefly, in the evening. I'd been wanting to speak to him about a particular comic book I was hoping to acquire. But he didn't have time to talk. He was totally focused on tracking down some or other jigsaw puzzle that he wanted to buy."

Luna opened her mouth to say that the puzzle Peter was working on right now was the one Robard had been so intent on acquiring. Then she closed it again. There was no need to broadcast that information to all and sundry.

Instead, she said, "A comic book? I didn't know that those were considered part of the games and hobby industry?"

"Some of our retailers still carry them, but comic books have become a specialized industry in their own right. Still, Paul told me he had a line on an *Avengers* comic from 1981 that I've been trying to acquire for ages. It would round out the series for me, which of course would make it that much more valuable. He was in a rush last night, but I don't think he was trying to avoid me or anything."

"You don't?"

"No, I think he would have been keen to make the deal. Word on the street was that times were tough for him financially. But, like I say, he couldn't concentrate on anything besides this one puzzle that he was after."

Luna tapped her chin as though something had just occurred to her. "You would probably know the answer to this. I applied to join an internet chatroom for the hobby industry. They haven't replied yet. Why would that be?"

"Probably because you aren't known in the industry. The chances are that they may never reply. Your application might very well stay in limbo."

"Well, that's annoying."

Peter shrugged.

"It seems so strange that someone would murder Paul Robard," Luna went on. "Why do you think anyone would do that?"

He glanced at the door. "How would I know?"

"You must have thought about it. I mean, you must have a theory."

"All I know is that he had a complicated family situation. He talked about it often. If I were the police, I'd look into that, rather than into his line of work."

Peter held out a puzzle piece to Luna and asked her to place it in the far corner of the frame. She took it unthinkingly, only to drop it like a hot potato half a second later as she remembered. She wasn't quite quick enough.

A flash of light sparked between her fingers and the dropped puzzle piece glowed for a full second as it landed on the table. She thought Peter's eyes were going to start from their sockets.

"Did you see that? Did you see it? Like a weird glow."

Luna felt the blood rushing to her cheeks but managed to answer calmly. "See what?"

"That puzzle piece! It was glowing." Peter snatched it up and examined it closely.

"It must have been a trick of the light. It looks normal to me." Luna hated to gaslight him, but she couldn't tell him the truth. She barely understood the truth herself.

Chapter 11

*P*eter Pipstow didn't linger. He seemed reluctant to touch the puzzle pieces again and stepped away from the table. He browsed briefly in the hobby section before exiting the bookshop with the air of a man who is being pursued.

"He left in a hurry," Jim called from the permanent collection. "That wouldn't have anything to do with the flash of light I saw a few minutes ago, would it?"

Luna sighed. "Won't you come over here for a moment? I want to show you something."

Jim left his laptop and made his way through a series of interleading rooms to the non-fiction section. "It's getting stronger, you know."

"What is?"

"Your connection to the puzzle. That flash of light was brighter than anything you've produced so far. Why did you touch it?"

"It was an accident. He handed me a piece and I took it without thinking. I dropped it almost immediately, but not soon enough."

Jim looked thoughtful. "You don't think he was testing you by handing you that piece?"

"I don't think so. He nearly fell over when the light appeared. He clearly wasn't expecting it. In fact, he seemed spooked, and got out of here as quickly as he could."

"Hmm." Jim nodded. "Anyway, what did you want to show me?"

Luna picked up a pencil and used it to nudge the box closer to Jim. "Look at the picture on the box and compare it to what he managed to build of the puzzle. What do you notice?"

Jim took a moment to inspect the puzzle, glancing at the box from time to time for reference. "The pictures are similar, but not exactly the same. Just from the small part of the puzzle that has been completed, you can see that the signage above this shop here is slightly different to how it appears on the box. And then of course there's the bunting that several of the shops are displaying. That tells me the image on the puzzle dates from at least 1938 because the bunting was displayed in Moonstone Village only after war was declared."

"That's what he said too – Peter Pipstow."

"Who exactly was he?" asked Jim.

"He has a website selling hobby and games merchandise. He knew the victim but says he only spoke to him briefly last night. He also knows Mr. Blackstone. He and Paul Robard worked in his hobby store in Leeds as teenagers."

"I imagine it's a tight community. They probably all know each other."

"Yes, but the funny thing was that when Melinda asked the crowd if anyone recognized him last night, no-one came forward. It was only when I figured that Tina knew him that we finally got an identification for him."

Jim thought about this. "Remember what Blackstone said to us this morning? Robard seems to have fallen on hard times. It might be that he hasn't been an active member of the jigsaw puzzle set for a while now."

"Maybe," said Luna. "But the internet seems to think that he still owned a hobby store quite recently. I find it hard to believe that Mr. Blackstone didn't recognize him."

"What did that Pipstow character say when you asked him who he thought might have killed Paul Robard?"

Luna smiled. "How do you know I asked him that?"

"Because I know you. You recognize the value of asking a direct question. Sometimes you get a direct answer."

"True. He just said that Robard had a messed-up family situation and that the police should probably look into that. Which of course they are doing."

Jim reached for a puzzle piece and placed it where it belonged. Then he placed another one, and another one.

"Thanks for helping with the puzzle, but I don't want it to interfere with your work."

"I'm taking a break. I like puzzles – they relax me."

Seeing that he was happily occupied, Luna went back to unpacking her merchandise.

～

"Cheerio, boss. I'll be off then."

It was five o'clock and Harper was heading out the door.

"Wait a minute!" Luna said, trying not to sound panicky. "Can I ask you something before you go?"

Harper did a U-turn and returned to the coffee station.

"Of course. What's up?" She gave Luna a curious look. "What are you doing, by the way?"

"I'm trying to mix this liquid into a hand cream as Matilda suggested. But I can't get the two elements to mix properly. They keep separating."

"It's that old oil and water thing, isn't it?" said Harper. "The hand lotion you've chosen is probably too greasy. Maybe try one that's a plain aqueous cream. Those are water-based so it should be able to absorb more liquid."

Luna tried again using a jar of unscented aqueous cream. The results were much more successful.

"Look at that! It's mixing beautifully. Thank you."

"Was that what you wanted to ask me?" asked Harper.

"Not exactly. I wanted to ask what you would wear to go out for dinner with this lady." Luna found a recent picture of Lady Kelvin on her phone and showed it to Harper.

"Blimey. She's scary well dressed, isn't she? Who is she?"

"That's Lady Kelvin."

"Lady ...? Oh, you mean Jim's mum. She's never invited you to dinner, has she?"

"Not just me and her alone, thank goodness. Jim and his sister will also be there. We're having dinner at the Grand Hotel."

"Urgh. That's kind of a stuffy place. It's all snail forks and finger bowls and linen napkins."

"So I gather."

"Do you want to hear what I'm doing this evening? My friends and I are going to that new build-your-own-burger place on the pier and then we're taking our burgers to eat on the beach. We might even light a fire."

Luna felt a wave of envy. Burgers on the beach with friends sounded absolutely perfect. If it had been just her,

Jim, and Bernie, that's exactly what she would have suggested. But Lady Kelvin was the complicating factor.

"Stop trying to make me jealous," said Luna. "Help me decide what I'm going to wear tonight."

Harper gave her a critical look. "Not your usual jeans-and-jumper combination, I would say."

Luna rolled her eyes. She was rather fond of wearing jeans and a sweater to work every day, but that wasn't her entire wardrobe. "Obviously not. I need to wear something smart."

"Do you own such a thing as a dress?"

"A couple, I guess. We had to wear them every night when I worked on the cruise ships."

"There you go then." Harper nodded. "A dress with heels and a lick of makeup. Wear your hair up and put on some very non-flashy jewelry. Lady What's-Her-Name will love you. Now, I'm going to meet my friends for a pint before we hit the burger place. See you tomorrow, boss."

Harper gave her a sustaining pat on the shoulder before heading for the door and disappearing into the pearly twilight.

Luna closed the shutters over the coffee serving hatch and locked the front door, turning the OPEN sign to CLOSED.

"Are you still guarding the puzzle?" she asked the cat. "You can stop now."

He stretched hugely and jumped off the table. Then he trotted up to see what she was doing in the kitchen area.

Luna smoothed some of the aqueous cream mixture over her hands. She concentrated on the fingertips, which would have the most contact with the puzzle pieces. Then she went back to the table in the non-fiction section to try out her new charm.

"Okay, let's see." She picked up a piece of the puzzle and held it aloft. For a second, nothing happened. Then it began to glow faintly. She showed the cat. "That's better, but still not perfect. I'll make the mixture stronger. More of the blocking charm and less of the aqueous cream."

She adjusted the quantities, whipping the mixture together for longer to force the cream to absorb the liquid. Then she applied it again and picked up another puzzle piece. This time there was no breakthrough glow. The puzzle piece remained perfectly ordinary and unglowy.

"Eureka," muttered Luna.

It was almost time to start getting ready for dinner, but she couldn't resist adding a few pieces to the puzzle. The fact that the picture on the box and the puzzle inside were not identical made it more challenging, but they were similar enough that the box provided a general guide.

The part of the puzzle that Luna worked on depicted an art deco storefront that must have been brand new at the time that the puzzle was made, and still remained the youngest architectural feature of the current High Street. If Luna was correct, it now housed a small flower shop, with Harper's aunt's real estate agency next door.

As the doorway and storefront slowly took form, it became clear that this was another one of the subtle differences between puzzle and box. The original store front was narrow, dark, and Victorian. The 1930s version was wider and brighter. It seemed to have been the home of a shop that sold bells for bicycles.

Luna stared at it for a long time, hoping that some kind of insight would strike her. Paul Robard had gone to great lengths to purchase this particular puzzle. It was his last significant act before he died. There must have been a reason he had wanted it so badly.

Nothing jumped out at her, so she went upstairs to get ready.

"The puzzle isn't a red herring, is it?" she asked the cat as she decanted a pouch of salmon in gravy into a bowl for him.

His answering meow had more to do with his eagerness for the food than with her question. He flung himself on the bowl the moment she put it down.

"No," she said. "It's not a red herring. I know it's important – I just don't know why."

She flung open the doors to her closet and rifled through the dresses she had collected during her time working on cruise ships. Some were pretty. Some were even stylish, but they all had a slight sheen to them – a touch of glitz that had seemed very appropriate within the cruise ship environment, that now looked vulgar in the pearly light of Moonstone Island. She would rather, she decided, be boiled in oil than appear in front of Lady Kelvin in one of those.

The alternatives were a couple of pretty floral cotton dresses that screamed 'daytime' and would not pass muster at the Grand Hotel. For a desperate moment, Luna considered trying to dress them up with accessories, but they had a cottagey, peasant-dress look that simply did not translate into evening.

Almost panicking now, Luna fired off an emergency SOS message by text.

Chapter 12

*D*etective Sergeant Melinda Knight arrived twenty minutes later bearing three garment bags still on their hangers. Luna was deeply impressed.

"You keep your dresses in garment bags?" She closed the door behind her friend and ushered her upstairs. "I knew I was asking the right person."

"I only use the bags for items I don't wear frequently. Stops them from getting dusty." Melinda threw the garment bags on Luna's bed and unzipped the top one. "Here, try this one. It's a classic LBD with a slightly nineteen-twenties flapper look to it. It has spaghetti straps and a dropped waist."

Pressed for time, Luna flung off her sweatshirt and jeans and stepped into the dress that Melinda held out for her. But no sooner had Melinda done up the zipper than she shook her head.

"No. This one's no good. Very unflattering. It works on me because I've got more of a straight-up-and-down figure. We're the same size, but you're more of an hourglass and I'm more of an ironing board."

Luna tutted as Melinda undid the zipper. "You're not an ironing board. You have a lovely figure."

"Don't get me wrong – I like my figure. But what suits me doesn't necessarily suit you. You need something that nips you in at the waist."

She held up the next dress. "This is more va-va-voom."

Luna eyed the new contender dubiously. It was a cock-tail-length dress in a fire-engine red. It was strapless, with a sweetheart neckline, and very form fitting.

As Melinda zipped it up, Luna turned towards the mirror and recoiled. "Wow. No, that's way too much va-va-voom."

Melinda gave her a critical look and nodded. "You're right. You look amazing, but it's too much for the Grand Hotel. We don't want to give Mrs. Jim a heart attack."

"Lady Kelvin. And you're right. What's left? I need to leave in about ten minutes."

Melinda opened the final garment bag. "This dress was officially a Mistake. I've nearly got rid of it half a dozen times. The color kills me stone dead. I only brought it tonight because I thought it might go with your red hair."

Luna stepped into the dress and waited for Melinda to do it up before turning towards the mirror.

"Hmm."

It was a deceptively simple linen-mixture shift dress. It was subtly tailored to accentuate the waist and ended just above the knee. The color was indeed difficult, being a dull grey-green that would drain the life out of most complexions. But somehow it worked on Luna. Her pale skin, dark eyes, and flaming red hair looked just fine against the dull green.

"I think this is the one."

"Agreed." Melinda plucked a bit of fluff off her shoulder.

"I can't believe how much better it looks on you than on me. It's lovely, but understated enough to please Mrs. Jim. I should just give it to you outright."

"No, you can't do that. It's fully lined and beautifully tailored. It can't have been cheap."

"We'll do a trade. You give me something out of your wardrobe that doesn't suit you and we'll call it even."

"Deal." Luna could think of at least three candidates off the top of her head. She turned this way and that, admiring herself in the mirror. "Yes, this is the one."

"I agree. So, are Mrs. Jim and sister-of-Jim staying at the Grand Hotel?"

Luna shook her head. "No, they always stay at Jim's B&B, apparently. It's just that Lady Kelvin likes to dine at the Grand."

"You know who else might be there tonight?"

Luna glanced at her. "Who?"

"Well, they're certainly staying there. They might have dinner somewhere else, of course."

"I still don't know who you're talking about."

"I'm telling you. Paul Robard's biological sister, Tina Kitson, is staying there and tonight she is being joined by her mother."

"Her mother? Really? That's Paul's biological mother, right?"

"That's right. But Tina tells me she's not coming because her biological son has been killed. She is only coming to give Tina moral support because she is upset about it. The father refused to come at all because he's angry at Tina for seeking out her long-lost brother."

"Charming. I wonder if I'll run into them."

"You can also keep an eye out for Paul's adoptive family," said Melinda. "They've checked into the Grand too. His mother, father, and adoptive brother. I've made an appointment to speak to them tomorrow. At least they seem genuinely upset about his passing."

Luna's eyebrows rose. "I foresee an awkward meeting if the adoptive family and the biological family run into each other over the aperitifs. I don't feel like breaking up any fights."

"Let's hope it doesn't come to that." Melinda looked at her in the mirror. "You can stick with those earrings, if you like, but put on a small pendant. Hair up and a touch of lipstick and you're good to go." She scooped up the rejected dresses and wrestled them into their bags. "My work here is done. Don't come down to see me out. I'll make sure the door latches properly behind me. Good luck with the Cooke family tonight."

Luna thanked her repeatedly before turning back to the mirror and scooping up a handful of hairpins.

"What do you think, Pyewacket? Melinda really came through, didn't she? I'll have to choose something that will look great on her for our exchange."

The cat looked pointedly at the clock on the wall.

"Yes, yes. Five minutes left before I need to leave, I know. I'll make it on time, you'll see."

She put up her hair with the ease of long practice, swiped on a discreet lick of lipstick, slid her feet into nude pumps with a moderate heel and let herself out the front door barely a minute later than she had planned.

~

The walk to the Grand Hotel was just long enough to remind Luna that she had forgotten how to walk in heels. She turned her ankle over three times before she finally found her balance and remembered that she used to walk on a swaying cruise ship in higher heels than these.

She managed the last few steps to the hotel with creditable steadiness. The Cookes were nowhere to be seen. But when a waiter ushered her into the dining room, they were all there, already seated at their table.

Jim jumped up to greet Luna with a kiss on the cheek. Then he turned to his mother.

"Mum, I'd like you to meet Luna Larkspur. Luna, this is my mother, Eliza Cooke."

Luna murmured, "How do you do?" and shook the cool, slender hand that was being held out to her.

"I hope I'm not late," she added as she sat down between Jim and Bernie.

"Not at all," said Jim. "We were early. I hope you don't mind that we ordered the three-course set menu. It's clear soup, followed by roast chicken and pudding."

Mentally translating 'pudding' into 'dessert', Luna smiled. "That sounds perfect."

"You're very polite," grumbled Bernie. "But it's rude to order for other people, and so I told Mum."

Lady Kelvin sniffed. "Nonsense, Bernadette. It's the perfect meal. Anyone would be pleased to eat it. And here's our soup now."

As a waiter distributed bowls of soup, Luna decided that the jury was still out on whether she needed to have panicked so much about what to wear. Lady Kelvin wore a peacock blue suit with discreet diamond earrings. Bernadette wore exactly the same dress she had been wearing all day. She hadn't bothered with lipstick and didn't even seem to have brushed her hair. Jim had added a tie and a darker than usual jacket to his regular outfit.

Luna reckoned that she fell somewhere in between Lady Kelvin and Bernie, which was fine.

"You look nice," said Jim, apparently reading her thoughts.

"Just what I was thinking," said Bernie. "You scrub up well, old girl."

"Thanks. You all look very nice too. But I can't take credit for this dress. It's Melinda's."

Lady Kelvin perked up. "That would be Melinda Knight, the police detective?"

"Mum loves a good murder mystery," said Bernie. "You can't drag her away from *Midsomer Murders* when it's on."

"Nonsense, Bernadette. If I happen to notice that it's on, I might watch for a little while. That's all."

"You mean you set the kitchen timer so that you never miss it," muttered Bernie.

Lady Kelvin ignored her. She turned to Luna. "James told me that you were friendly with D.S. Knight. It must be so interesting to hear her talk about her cases."

"It is," said Luna. "Mind you, she mostly complains about her kids when we're together. Moonstone Island isn't exactly a hub of international crime. But she does have rather an interesting case at the moment."

Lady Kelvin leaned forward, her eyes shining. "Tell me."

Luna spooned up some more of her soup. "A man by the name of Paul Robard was killed at the jigsaw puzzle convention at the Scout Hall last night. He was struck from behind with a heavy object."

"Did his attacker definitely mean to kill him?" asked Lady Kelvin. "Or just disable him? That makes a big difference."

"It does indeed. I don't think the police are sure either way yet." Luna opened her mouth to give more details when a sudden outbreak of raised voices drew everyone's attention.

She looked up to locate the source of the ruckus. Then she said under her breath, "Oh, dear."

It was Tina Kitson. She had entered the dining room in the company of an older woman who looked so unmistakably like her that it had to be her mother. Both ladies were visibly upset.

"Why did you bother to come?" demanded Tina. "Did you just want to upset me?"

The older woman rolled her eyes. "Don't be ridiculous, Tina. And keep your voice down. You're making a scene."

"I don't care," hissed Tina. "Respectability. Everlasting respectability. You've preached it to me my whole life."

"Well, it doesn't seem to have worked."

Before the ladies could get any louder, a waiter ushered them to their table.

Chapter 13

*W*hen the soup bowls had been cleared, Jim leaned forward and lowered his voice. "Isn't that the sister of the chap who was killed?"

"That's his biological sister, yes," said Luna. "They didn't grow up together. When Paul was born, his parents gave him up for adoption because, according to the sister, it wasn't the right time in their lives for them to have a child. Two years later, she was born, and they kept her. She was fascinated by her absent brother and tracked him down in adulthood. They were going to meet face to face for the first time on the night he died."

Lady Kelvin's face fell. "Does that mean they never got a chance to meet, to talk to each other?"

"That's what Tina says – the sister. Obviously, the police are trying to confirm that. But they had been corresponding by email for quite some time."

"So, let me get this straight," said Bernie. "The parents gave their first baby up for adoption, but kept the next one that came along two years later?"

"Correct."

"Were they having financial trouble?"

"Apparently not. The way Tina tells it, her parents hadn't planned to have a baby for another couple of years, so they gave him up for adoption."

"Hmm."

"Tina says she spent her childhood afraid of misbehaving in any way in case her parents decided to send her away. But that's her perspective. I'm sure if you spoke to the parents, you'd get a different point of view."

Bernie shot a glance at the table where Tina and her mother sat in offended silence. "Things seem to be pretty tense between them."

"According to Melinda, the mother came to offer moral support to her daughter."

"Really?" said Lady Kelvin. "I wouldn't say it's going very well."

Lady Kelvin had one of those loud, aristocratic voices that carried across a crowded room. It was time to change the subject.

"How did you get on with the wedding shopping today?" Luna asked as the waiter deposited plates of crispy roast chicken, roast potatoes, and green beans in front of them.

"It went really well," said Lady Kelvin with a nod. "I found the perfect mother-of-the-bride outfit. It's vintage, dating from the sixties. I got it from my friend Viola's shop. She always knows exactly what I'll like and, more importantly, what will suit me."

"And I'm pretty sure I've found my dress," said Bernie. "Mum and I both love it. I even found the exact roll of taffeta that Flora wants to make her own dress. She's very practical, my wife to be."

"Yes, she is." Lady Kelvin reached out a narrow hand and touched her daughter on the wrist. It was a gesture of support, of the kind that was lacking at the table where the Kitson women sat. Luna caught a glimpse of Jim's face as he watched his mother and sister. It glowed with love and pride. He adored these women and the way they were with each other, she realized.

No one who hoped to get close to Jim could do so without the approval of his nearest and dearest. And while Bernie was certainly friendly, Lady Kelvin was quite reserved.

Not that it mattered to her, Luna told herself. Her primary duty was to Moonstone Island. She had to fill the big shoes left by her ancestor, Coco Larkspur. It was a daunting task, and one that was unlikely to leave time for a relationship.

And so she retreated from the task of trying to win Lady Kelvin over and decided just to enjoy the meal for its own sake.

∽

As the main course came to an end, the noise level at the Kitson table began to rise again.

"Oh, dear," said Lady Kelvin. "I'm afraid they really are going to cause a scene unless someone steps in."

"Don't you even care that he had a miserable life?" demanded Tina. "The family that you gave him to didn't keep him. They returned him to the adoption agency like he was a ... a jacket that didn't fit properly. He went into the foster system. He had a hellish time."

Her mother shook her head. "We didn't place him with those people, the adoption agency did. It wasn't our fault. And obviously in those days they didn't keep us apprised of every development in his life. That was the whole point of a closed adoption. He was no longer our child. In fact, he was never our child. From the moment we declared our intention to put him up for adoption, he had nothing to do with us."

"He was your flesh and blood!" Tina was close to yelling now.

"By an accident of birth, no more."

"Don't you even care that he's dead?"

"Keep your voice down, Christina. You sound hysterical. Of course I care that he's dead. I would be sorry to hear that any young man of forty had passed away, especially in violent circumstances. And this is why I am here, after all. I know you are upset, and I have come to offer you my support."

"Well, all you're doing is upsetting me."

Mother and daughter lapsed into silence.

Bernie rolled her eyes. "That mother is just awful. I'm Team Tina, for sure."

"She certainly seems like a cold fish," said Luna. "But I still think we don't know enough to judge."

The waiter distributed bowls of cinnamon rice pudding for dessert and brought a cheese board to the table.

Lady Kelvin's smiled. "Pudding *and* cheese. You see why I always choose to dine here?"

Bernie winked at Jim. "Mum has her cheese board. All is right with the world."

"Glass of port to go with that, Mum?" asked Jim.

Lady Kelvin suppressed a smile. "Now, James. You know I don't partake. I will finish my glass of wine instead."

The argument at the Kitson table flared up again.

"Why isn't he here?" asked Tina. "His son is dead. The least he can do is come and pay his respects. It's not like poor Paul is in a position to make any demands on him."

Her mother muttered something that sounded like, "Not anymore."

Tina pounced on this. "What is that supposed to mean?"

"Nothing."

"No, you said it for a reason. What do you mean, not anymore? When did he ever make demands on you or dad?"

Her mother sighed. "Your father and I didn't want to tell you this, Christina, but after you got in touch with Paul Robard, he used the information you gave him to track us down. He began emailing your father to ask him for money."

"I don't believe you." The shock on Tina's face convinced Luna that she hadn't known about this.

Her mother shrugged. "Have it your own way, but it's true. When your father refused, he threatened to sell his story to the media – how we cruelly gave him up for adoption and he was shunted from home to home before finally settling with the Robards."

"I don't believe it," whispered Tina.

"Well, it's still true. Naturally, your father wouldn't give way to blackmail, but the man became more and more desperate. He claimed he was on the trail of something that would make him an absolute fortune. Said he would pay your father back as soon as he got it. It was all nonsense, of course."

"What thing? What could he possibly have meant?"

Her mother shrugged again. "Some collector's item, I would imagine. Something related to his ridiculous hobby business. Your father didn't fall for it. But you can understand why he isn't here today."

Tina folded her arms across her chest. "So, he stayed home?"

Her mother hesitated for the first time. "As a matter of

fact, he's away at the moment. He has been for three days. Some last-minute business trip that came up."

Their voices dropped, making it difficult to hear what they were saying.

Luna couldn't even bring herself to feel ashamed of eavesdropping. The whole dining room was doing it, including the waiters. Every conversation had fallen silent as people strained to over-hear the mother and daughter.

Tina and her mother seemed oblivious of the entertainment they were providing. They were too wrapped up in their family drama to feel self-conscious.

Then Tina's voice rose again. "You! It's you."

Luna looked up to discover that Tina was looking right at her. A sinking feeling told her that she remembered exactly where she had seen Luna before.

Tina half-rose from the table. "You're the one who realized that I look like him – like Paul. You were there when the police questioned me."

"Sit down, Tina," hissed her mother.

"I will not sit down." She approached Luna's table. Luna felt herself blushing almost painfully under the scrutiny of the entire hotel dining room. She was aware of Lady Kelvin sitting between Jim and Bernie, her posture rigid.

When it became clear that Tina really was going to accost her in the middle of the dessert course, Luna stood up too.

"Let's take this outside, Tina. We can talk in the lobby. These folks don't want their dinner disturbed."

Tina was too far gone to listen. "Tell her!" She sliced the air, pointing at her mother. "Tell her it's suspicious that my father has been essentially missing for three days."

Her mother's jaw was so tightly clenched she almost couldn't speak. "Your father is not *missing*, Christina. I merely said I wasn't sure which town he is in at this exact moment. I know he's somewhere in the south-east. He moves around a lot. But he phones me every evening, like clockwork."

"But you admit that you don't know where he's been these last few days. He could be right here on Moonstone Island and none of us would know anything about it. You said Paul had been trying to extort money from him. That sounds like a motive for murder to me. Not everyone is as easily duped as you are, Mum."

"What utter nonsense, Christina. That man was no more than a nuisance to your father."

Tina took a deep breath and yelled so loudly the windows seemed to rattle. "That man was your son!"

Now that they were back in well-worn territory, her mother seemed to calm down. "He was not our son. Not legally, nor by any other metric that matters."

"He was your flesh and blood."

Her mother smiled as though humoring a child having a tantrum.

It was time to intervene before blood was shed.

"Let's step into the lobby," said Luna. "We can talk it all through there."

Luna knew she could calm Tina if she could only touch her. But any attempt to do so now would result in her getting decked.

Chapter 14

$\mathcal{M}$uttering an excuse to the Cookes, Luna led Tina out of the dining room and into the hotel lobby. She ushered her to a couch where they both sat down.

"You'll feel better in a moment," she said, resting the fingertips of one hand lightly against Tina's forearm.

"You're very kind," said Tina. "But I don't see how I can."

Luna waited for a feeling of warmth to tingle in her fingertips as she transferred comfort to Tina. But nothing happened.

For a mystified second, she wondered what was wrong. This had always worked in the past. She had always been able to impart a small measure of calm and comfort to an upset person through the medium of touch.

Then she remembered the lotion she had spread liberally over her hands earlier that evening and not washed off. The blocking charm was doing its job all too well.

Luna shifted her position on the couch until her elbow brushed against Tina's. They were once again skin to skin.

Aware that she probably looked like someone who didn't

have a good sense of physical boundaries, Luna ignored the slight inappropriateness of what she was doing and concentrated on slowing her breathing. Then she felt it.

A tingling warmth built up in her arm and passed from her body to Tina's.

The older woman slumped against the back of the couch as the tension left her body. "You're right. I do feel better."

Luna shifted sideways a few discreet inches, so she was now sitting at an appropriate distance. "I'm glad."

Tina blew out a sigh. "I don't know why I let them get to me like that – my parents, I mean. They can't help being who they are any more than I can. We've been having different versions of this same argument my whole life. Paul's death just brought it into focus."

"Are you really suspicious of your father?" asked Luna.

"I don't know. I mean, probably not, right? I didn't know that Paul was asking him for money. But that doesn't seem like a good enough reason to kill someone. The whole thing is just so sad. I wish it could have had a different ending."

"Did Paul never ask you for money at any stage?"

Tina gave a reluctant laugh. "No, but I think that's because he knew I didn't have any. I told him I had to save up for months to afford this trip to Moonstone Island. He did mention that there was something he wanted to talk to me about, so maybe he was working up to asking me for a few pounds."

"Do you have any idea what collector's item it was that he was after?"

"Not really. He mentioned some comic book or other, but I also know that he was anxious to get hold of a particular jigsaw puzzle. He was deliberately vague about the details."

"Why do you think that was?"

"He didn't trust me. I was part of his biological family, and, in his eyes, we had betrayed him. He only trusted the Robards."

Tina sat forward and rested her hands on her knees. "I'd better go back to my mother. Don't worry, we won't cause any more drama. We should probably go upstairs and order room service. Thanks for listening to me, and sorry for dragging you into our family business."

"That's quite all right."

Luna returned to the dining room and sat down at the Cookes' table. She had only been gone a few minutes but felt obliged to apologize again.

"Not to worry." Bernie waved her dessert spoon in the air. "Thanks for defusing the situation. I see they're going upstairs. That's probably best for everyone."

Luna shot a glance around the table. Had her disappearance in the middle of dessert been regarded as rude?

Bernie seemed to be her usual happy-go-lucky self and Jim appeared as calm and good-humored as ever. Lady Kelvin was harder to read. Luna hoped she hadn't committed some terrible breach of etiquette by leaving the room with Tina Kitson.

She picked up a spoon and began to eat her rice pudding. It was not her favorite dessert in the world. She suspected that it was one of those dishes you had to have grown up with in early childhood. Her first encounter with it had been as an adult on Moonstone Island, and she found it a bit sickly.

She had to admit, however, that the Grand Hotel's version was superior. It didn't have that slimy texture she usually found off-putting, and the flavors were complex and well-developed.

It was clear that real cinnamon sticks and vanilla bean pods had been used in the making of it, with pleasing results. When she finished the dessert, Jim passed her the cheese board and she sliced off a sliver of brie. Luna might never come to embrace rice pudding fully, but the British habit of ending a meal with a selection of cheeses had her full support.

Lady Kelvin signaled the waiter to bring the coffee before turning to Luna. "There's a calmness about you. Your grandfather had the same thing. I like it."

Trying not to look as surprised as she felt, Luna replied, "That's kind of you to say, but he and I share a tendency to a quick temper. Many would blame it on our red hair." She gave her head a rueful tap.

"That as may be," said Lady Kelvin. "But I'm not wrong about the calmness. That woman came in like a lion and you made her go out like a lamb. It's a rare talent."

"Her cat has the same quality," said Bernie. "Normally, Sir Lancelot gets restless when I'm not with him, but today he was perfectly content to hang out with Luna's cat while I went shopping. I'm tempted to kidnap your feline and take him home with me to be a permanent companion for my rooster."

Jim laughed. "Try it and you'll get a taste of that famous Larkspur temper."

Luna nodded. "Yes, I'm afraid Pyewacket stays where he is. He was my grandfather's cat and now he's mine. Or perhaps we are his. It's hard to tell with cats."

Bernie leaned forward, struck by an idea. "Jim should bring you to the farm some time. You and the cat. He can hang out with Sir Lancelot while we show you the farm and our whole operation."

"I would love that." Ever since Luna had heard about the

innovations Bernie had made on the Kelvin Manor estate, she had been dying to see it for herself.

"That settles it. Jim, bring the girl and bring her soon."

≈

As Luna got ready for bed that night, she was aware of being too hyped up to sleep.

Her brain had been flooded with new information about the case. There was only one way to calm her mind and that was to pass the information on. She interrupted her skin care routine to send a message to Melinda Knight with all the salient points.

She told her that Paul Robard had approached his biological father for money and that this had escalated to attempted blackmail. She also told her that the biological father was currently away from home and that not even his wife could say with any certainty where he was right now or where he had been on the night of Paul Robard's murder.

Afterwards, she felt calmer. She had done the right thing in passing on the information. Melinda would know what to do with it. It was no longer her sole responsibility.

But no sooner was that off her chest than she began to worry about her reaction to Bernie's invitation to see the Kelvin Manor farm.

Had she seemed too eager? She was genuinely excited to see everything she had heard about - the rare breeds program, the organic farm, the petting zoo, the shop. She was even keen to see the tearoom that was still under construction, and that was nothing but a pile of bricks at the moment. But perhaps her eagerness had sounded like something else. Perhaps it had made her sounded like an

American gold digger whose eyes lit up at the prospect of an aristocrat's estate.

She cringed at the memory of her own voice saying, "I would love that." Lady Kelvin would have seen straight through that to the avaricious heart that beat within her chest. The fact that she was genuinely not avaricious in the slightest didn't seem to matter. That's probably what they thought of her.

A sharp pain in her ankle made Luna squeal and almost drop her moisturizer.

"What was that for?" she demanded as the cat looked up at her after nipping her ankle. "You're supposed to save that for people who steal jigsaw puzzle pieces." He stared up at her, his pupils so large that his eyes appeared black.

"Okay, okay," she said. "I'm being ridiculous. I'm imposing my own insecurities on the Cookes and imagining them thinking things that they probably aren't thinking at all. I'll stop doing that now."

The cat rubbed his head against her ankle. It wasn't an apology so much as a reminder that he had easy access to her ankles if she went down the path of catastrophic thinking again.

Luna got into bed feeling tired, but not quite ready to sleep. Normally she would have dived straight into the romance novel that Bernie had recommended to her. But when she was in this mood, there was only one thing that helped – the diary of Coco Larkspur. It was the best cure for a troubled mind she had ever encountered.

She had tried reading it from cover to cover, but that never seemed to work. It was best to let the diary guide her. It was made for dipping into, not reading continuously. As the cat settled next to her, she paged through the diary, waiting for something to catch her eye.

"This looks like a good one," she told the sleepy cat. He purred and kneaded the comforter.

Do people really kill their nearest and dearest?

During my time on Moonstone Island, I have had occasion to work closely with the local police force from time to time. In my conversations with them, I have been surprised to learn that when a crime has been committed, the police are more suspicious of those closest to the victim than they are of strangers.

That seems odd, doesn't it? We are more accustomed to think of the thief in the night, or the nameless villain as the 'type' of person who commits a crime.

And of course that is true for many crimes. The thief who steals an apple from a fruit store is probably just hungry. The pickpocket who makes off with your wallet on a crowded street is probably unknown to you. Even the murderer who stabs you for your pearl necklace probably has nothing against you personally.

But my conversations with police officers have recently convinced me that many crimes have more personal motivations. People are driven to commit crimes because of a range of emotions, including jealousy, resentment, revenge, hatred, envy, and spite. It is difficult to feel those emotions for someone you don't know well. Those emotions take time and intimacy to develop.

Another lesson I have learnt is that people will kill if they believe that something of theirs is threatened. This could be a possession, a relationship, or their status and reputation. If these are threatened, people will go to great lengths to protect what they value.

I hope these musings may be helpful. I am no more than an

unlettered beginner in such matters myself. But I am learning and perhaps you can learn with me.

"She has a point, as usual," Luna muttered as she closed the diary. "I don't think any of us thought that the murder of Paul Robard was a random act. But what was the motivation?

The cat purred lazily as she tickled his back.

"Was it a crime of strong emotion by someone who knew him well, or was it someone who felt threatened by him? Or something else altogether? We need to think carefully about this."

Soothed at last, Luna fell deeply asleep.

Chapter 15

*S*he was woken up five minutes before her alarm was due to go off by her phone ringing.

As it buzzed and vibrated on her nightstand, she rolled over and buried her head in the pillow.

"Go 'way," she mumbled. "I'm sleeping."

But the phone continued to buzz, and the cat tapped her on the cheek with his paw until she groaned and sat up.

A spike of adrenalin cleared her head when she saw that it was Melinda Knight. She snatched up the phone.

"Hello?"

"Sorry, Luna. I know it's early. Marcus Blackstone's stall was raided overnight."

"Marcus ...?" Luna's head cleared some more as the significance of the name hit her. "Oh, him. What did they take?"

"That's what we're trying to establish. I thought you might like to come and see."

All thoughts of snuggling back into bed left Luna's head. "I'll be there in ten minutes."

By the time she had leapt into the shower, flung on her

clothes, scooped food into a bowl for the cat, and sprinted up Seagull Lane, it was more like fifteen minutes. She arrived at the Scout Hall puffing for breath and feeling as though she had started her day by being shot out of a cannon.

It was just shy of six-thirty. The High Street still dozed in an early-morning slumber. The shopfronts were closed. The only sign of life came from a restaurant that opened for breakfast at seven o'clock. A light was on, and the staff milled about inside getting ready for the day.

Melinda's car was parked in front of the Scout Hall. The main doors were firmly shut, but Luna could see where the break-in had occurred. A pair of side doors had been forced open. One was slightly buckled, with a splinter of wood showing the point of impact.

Not wanting to disturb any evidence gathering that might be going on, Luna approached the gaping doors carefully. Melinda waved her in.

"Come on over, but don't touch anything. My scene-of-crime officers are on their way."

Luna stepped carefully into the hall, noting that everything was still in place for the ongoing jigsaw puzzle convention. Most of the stallholders had left their wares out for the next day. Some had draped drop-cloths over them. As far as Luna could see, only one had been disturbed. The stall belonging to Marcus Blackstone had been extensively rifled. A number of puzzle boxes were opened, and their pieces strewn on the floor. Plastic wrapping had been slashed apart and discarded on the table and on the floor.

Marcus Blackstone stood by the stall, next to PC Cooper. It was clear that he too had been told not to touch anything. Instead, he swiped through images on his tablet, apparently comparing them with what was left on the table. He seemed to be taking inventory in an attempt to establish if anything had been stolen.

Mindful of what Melinda had called her here for, Luna stepped up to greet him. "I'm so sorry this has happened, Mr. Blackstone. It must be distressing for you to see your stall in this condition."

He gave her a narrow look. "Oh, it's you, is it? The one who bought the vintage, hand-cut street scene of Moonstone Village. What are you doing here?"

"I'm a friend of DS Knight's. She asked me to help you establish the extent of the damage and whether anything was taken."

He frowned as he glanced at his tablet. "I haven't found anything missing yet, which is strange because the motive must have been burglary."

"What are your most valuable items?"

"Those would be the limited-edition hand-cut puzzles like the one you bought. But as far as I can see, those are all here. They are worth a few hundred pounds each. Other individual items are worth much less than that."

"What about vandalism?" asked Luna. "Motivated by spite, perhaps."

"In that case, they didn't do a very good job, did they? This is hardly a case of wholesale destruction. It will take me an hour or so to put everything back to the way it was. Someone who was serious about vandalism could have done much more damage than this."

Luna had to acknowledge that he was right. The person who had been through his stock was certainly careless, but not necessarily malicious.

"If you had to guess who was responsible for this, who would your top candidate be?"

He shrugged. "Perhaps a competitor? It has to have been

someone who was trying to damage my business in some way. But this is a very niche selection of my overall business. I trade in hobby items of all kinds."

"So jigsaw puzzles aren't your particular focus?" asked Luna.

"Not at all. But I've learned from experience that it's best to come to a convention like this with a particular theme. I make better sales than I would if I displayed a mixed selection."

"Is it possible that the person who tossed your store was looking for something specific?"

"I'm starting to think so, yes. But I have no idea what that might be. As I say, I haven't found anything missing yet."

He turned away from her. But Luna wasn't finished with him yet.

"Mr. Blackstone," said Luna as he flicked through the list of stock on his tablet.

He looked up irritably. "Yes, young lady. What is it? I'm a trifle distracted right now, as you might imagine."

"When I asked you whether you had ever seen Paul Robard, the man who was murdered here two nights ago, you denied it."

"Yes. So?"

"So, he worked at your hobby store in Leeds as a teenager. You must have known who he was."

Blackstone sighed and shook his head. But even as he exuded exasperation, Luna suspected that this was a performance. This information was not new to him and there was an edge of nervousness underlying his behavior.

"That must have been more than twenty years ago, young lady," he said. "I didn't know every spotty-faced teenager who worked for me in those days. And I certainly wouldn't remember one after such a long time."

"But he would have remembered you, Mr. Blackstone. Surely he reminded you of the connection when you spoke to him on the night he died?"

Blackstone made an impatient sound. "He addressed me in an overly familiar way. I thought he was just a rude man. I didn't realize that I'd met him before. I knew the other Robard boy much better, in any event."

Luna tried not to look as interested as she felt. "The other Robard boy?"

"Yes, they both worked in my shop at one time or another. I knew the older one better. I believe his name was Ellis."

"They were brothers?"

"Sort of. They were – what do you call it – foster brothers. They looked nothing alike and were several years apart. Ellis Robard was more memorable. He had one of those big personalities. I had no trouble recognizing him when I saw him again."

"When was that, Mr. Blackstone?"

"That was last night. He was out and about in the village at the same time as I was."

"I see." Luna remembered Melinda mentioning that Paul Robard's adoptive parents and brother were due to arrive on the island the day before. They were also staying at the Grand Hotel.

Blackstone swiped his tablet again. "If you don't mind, I'd like to get on with trying to establish which items of my stock have been damaged or stolen."

∽

It was just after seven o'clock when Luna walked back home. The island began to wake up as the sun crept over the eastern horizon.

Luna texted as she walked, filling Melinda in on everything she had learned from her conversation with Marcus Blackstone. She had a strong suspicion about what the intruder had been looking for from the Blackstone stall. Her conscience wouldn't allow her to keep it to herself, much as she wanted to.

I have to tell you that Blackstone and I came to the same conclusion – that the intruder targeted his stall because he was looking for something. And since Blackstone can't seem to find any missing stock, it seems the intruder failed to find whatever he was looking for. Can't help thinking he was looking for the same thing as Paul Robard – my jigsaw puzzle. If you think it's better off in police custody, I'll understand.

Luna added a string of crying emojis and broken heart emojis to show that while she would understand having to give up her puzzle, she wasn't at all happy about it.

A moment later, her phone buzzed with Melinda's reply.

Nah, you can keep it for now. From what you were saying, it has some kind of hocus pocus attached to it. That's more in your wheelhouse than mine. As long as you're aware that this is a small island and word WILL get out that you have the puzzle. If you're comfortable with that risk, you can keep it. Just try to get it built so we can see if it contains a clue.

Exhaling slowly with relief, Luna replied.

Will try my hardest.

Her biggest clue wasn't about to be taken away from her, and that was good news.

She had arrived at Charmed. As usual, she felt a little spurt of pride and disbelief that it was actually hers. She had done nothing to earn it, but she would make very sure that she did everything possible to keep her family's legacy alive. She would earn it retrospectively.

Speaking of which, she couldn't help noticing that her window display looked a little thin. It was three days' old already and in need of refreshing. The theme had been 'Westerns'. She had found piles of Zane Grey novels, piles of Louis L'Amour novels and sprinkled them with Larry McMurtry and Cormac McCarthy. If a book had been made into a movie, she gave it pride of place.

She had decorated the display with an old saddle she had found in the attic, a pair of fake cowboy boots, and a ten-gallon hat she found at the party store.

The promotion had obviously done well because only a few Zane Greys and Louis L'Amours were left. It was time for a new theme, and luckily Luna had some ideas about that.

She let herself into the store and switched on the lights.

"Yes, I'm back," she greeted Pyewacket as he trotted up to meet her. "No, you're not getting a second breakfast, so don't even think about it. You can eat your dry food until it's time for dinner."

The cat flipped over, lifted his leg, and washed his tummy energetically, as though no thoughts of a second breakfast had ever entered his head.

Slightly paranoid after Melinda's text, Luna checked on the puzzle. It seemed to be all in order. In a moment, she would put on her blocking hand cream and make some progress with it. But first, she needed to attend to the window display.

Chapter 16

*I*n a recent shipment of almost-new releases, Luna had received several books that fell into the self-help category. There were a couple by Brené Brown, Esther Perel, and Deepak Chopra. There weren't enough of them to fill out a display on their own, but Luna was confident of finding more books with a similar theme on her second-hand shelves to create an attractive show.

She searched the non-fiction shelves until she had found a decent pile of vintage Dale Carnegie, Stephen R Covey, Eckhart Tolle, Victor Frankl, and Susan Jeffers. She arranged them attractively on the stands in her window display, with the newer books to the fore. She draped some bolts of fabric in fall colors around the stand and trotted up to her apartment to see which herbs were having an autumnal flowering. Her lavender and fennel looked pretty so she arranged them as extra color in the window display. She had been about to pinch off the flowers from the fennel to discourage it from going to seed, but that could wait a while. It was too useful as a window decoration.

When the self-help display had run its course, Luna

decided, she would go full Halloween with a display of horror novels. She would also think about decorating the whole store for Halloween. The holiday wasn't nearly as big here in the UK as it was back home in America, but she fully intended to fling herself into the spooky spirit.

Kids were kids all over the world and if her spooky decorations encouraged them to force their parents into her store, that was all to the good. Luna added 'Buy Halloween decorations' to the to-do list she kept on her phone. Then she washed her hands and carefully applied a thick layer of the blocking cream. She had half an hour to before she had to open the serving hatch for coffee sales, and she intended to use it to build the puzzle.

Practice made perfect when it came to jigsaw puzzles, Luna discovered. When she had first worked on this puzzle, she had wasted a lot of time staring at the unplaced pieces, waiting for something to jump out at her. Now she was more active, seeking out specific color synchronicities and tiny details that gave a clue as to where something belonged.

The main thing that struck Luna as she made progress with the puzzle was how little the high street of Moonstone Village had changed over the years. The box showed a street scene from the nineteen-twenties, the puzzle showed the same street scene from the late nineteen-thirties, and she knew the High Street of the twenty-first century. Shops had changed hands, signage was very different, and the cars and people's clothes were unrecognizably different. But the basic bone structure of the street remained the same. Luna knew that the village council kept a tight lid on architectural changes in the village – especially the older and more historical parts of it. Most of the buildings in the High Street were listed. You practically needed written permission to put up a flyer. There were other parts of the island where you were a lot freer to build and demolish at will, but not in the original, historical village.

This continuity meant that any clue the puzzle might yield had a small chance of still being relevant today. It was a very small chance, Luna admitted. The buildings might still be the same, but generations had come and gone since 1938. Bicycle shops had become cellphone repair stores. A stamp-collecting emporium had become the party shop that she intended to go Halloween shopping at.

One of the few Moonstone Village institutions that was still the same as it had ever been was Charmed Bookstore. And that was located down on Beach Road – nowhere near the High Street.

With an exclamation of triumph, Luna located the piece she had been looking for. It was the very top of the church steeple. As she turned it the right way round and pressed it into place, it began to glow slightly. Her blocking cream was wearing off and whatever strange connection she had to this puzzle had reasserted itself.

Tutting with annoyance, she contemplated reapplying the cream. But Pyewacket tapped her on the leg, and she glanced at the wall clock. It was almost eight o'clock. Time to boot up the coffee machine and open her shutters to the waiting public.

Feeling as though she had already done a full day's work, Luna went to start caffeinating the masses.

∾

"Look at that!" said Harper as she arrived for work an hour later. "You've made great progress with the puzzle."

"It's become a priority now," said Luna. "Melinda Knight

said she's happy to leave it with me, but only if I get on with finishing it."

Harper gave the puzzle a longing look. "I'd love to have a crack at it. I'm really good at puzzles. We always have one on the go at Christmas time – even bigger than this one sometimes."

"I wish you would," said Luna. "Like I said, it's the priority."

"I can't leave the coffee station. We've become too popular. Hardly ten minutes go by without a new customer."

"I'll man the coffee station. If you could make progress with the puzzle, that'd be great."

"Excellent." Rubbing her hands together, Harper stationed herself in the non-fiction section and turned her attention to the puzzle.

Luna split her focus between the coffee station and the rest of the bookstore, which formally opened at nine. The first sale of the day was a book from her self-help display. At least that proved that it was attracting attention.

"Someone sold you a dud," called Harper. "The picture on the puzzle and the picture on the box are not the same."

"That might turn out to be the whole point," said Luna. "The man who died, Paul Robard, wanted this exact puzzle specifically. It's a limited series puzzle and he wanted this exact one. I guess when we're finished building it, we'll figure out why."

"I noticed something else a little odd," said Harper.

"What's that?"

"The image on the box shows a series of trees in pots that have been trimmed into different shapes. Like a square and a circle and a triangle and so on. It's - what do you call it - topiary."

"Yes, I noticed that."

"Well, one of the trees in the puzzle is not a triangle, but the letter B."

Luna abandoned the coffee station to see the puzzle for herself.

"Wow, yes. Look at that. It's clearly a capital B." She looked up as Jim entered, swinging his laptop bag in one hand, and carrying a pile of files in the other. She waved him over. "Come and look at this. Harper has found another difference between the puzzle and the box."

Jim studied the puzzle, then consulted the box, then turned back to the puzzle. "Intriguing. I wonder if each one of the pot plants represents a different letter of the alphabet. Maybe they spell out something."

"It's impossible to tell from the puzzle pieces," said Harper. "They're too small. Each one shows a bit of dark green foliage. It's only when you put them together that you see that the tree has suddenly turned into a letter."

Thoughts whirled through Luna's mind. "Do you think there is any chance that the High Street of 1938 really featured topiary bushes that had been trimmed into the shape of letters of the alphabet?"

Jim shook his head. "Highly unlikely. I'm not aware of any such fad."

Harper shook her head too. "I've been Googling it. There are old photographs of the trees trimmed into shapes, but not into letters."

"Then they were added to the puzzle for a reason," said Luna. "We need to get all those pots built to see what they spell, if anything."

Jim put his laptop and files down in the permanent collection. "So, while the two of you hover over the puzzle, who do I ask for a cup of coffee and a cookie?"

Harper hurried over to the coffee hatch where some

customers were already waiting. "I'll do it. My half hour is up. I know your dastardly plan, Jim Cooke. You want a crack at that puzzle yourself."

Jim flexed his fingers and grinned. "You're right, I do."

As Harper prepared a latte and a white chocolate chip cookie for Jim, and Jim eased into his working morning by spending twenty minutes on the jigsaw puzzle, Luna caught up with her admin. She had bills to pay, salary slips to prepare (she paid herself a monthly salary, as well as Harper), and orders to get out. She ran through huge amounts of coffee beans, creamer, flavored syrups, and toppings every month. She had also recently started purchasing her baking ingredients from a wholesaler. It was just too expensive to pop to the supermarket and purchase what she needed at retail prices.

Luna had also recently contracted with a cleaning service to come into the bookstore once a week after hours to give it a good clean. That old-book smell was all very well, but when it became overlaid with dust and must, Luna drew the line. The cleaning company had sorted that out, thank goodness.

She and Harper kept the coffee station spotless with regular cleaning every day, but the many rooms of the large bookstore were a challenge.

It was an extra monthly expense, but so far she didn't regret it. It was worth it to have the wood paneling gleaming with lemon furniture polish and the thick, old carpets freshly hoovered. Even the drapes looked brighter now that they had been taken down, professionally laundered, and rehung.

Yes, her expenses had gone up, but her income had too. She wouldn't quite break even this month, but she would come close. And if November wasn't the month that she finally made it into the black, she had high hopes for December. She had plans for a line of festive beverages and cookies, and a display of children's books and toys. December, she decided, would be the month she finally started turning a profit.

But that was for the future. She was still concerned about October and how to leverage Halloween season to get more people into the store.

Luna updated her social media feeds – posting photographs of her self-help display to Instagram and to her other platforms. She dashed off a couple of paragraphs of text about the evolution of self-help books and the explosion of podcasts in the field.

No sooner had she posted her updates than she got a private message from Bernie Cooke. *'Post the cat and rooster pics from yesterday!'*

Chapter 17

*I*t was a lightbulb moment.

Luna scrolled through her camera roll and saw that of course she had taken at least a dozen pictures of Pyewacket with his new BFF Sir Lancelot. She had done it for her own enjoyment, not for social media. But now she could see that several of the pictures were extremely Instagram-worthy.

Bernie had built the whole Kelvin Manor brand around her adorable tame rooster. And that had netted her a few hundred thousand followers. She was obviously doing something right.

Leaving her previous post as it was, Luna created a new post with a photo dump of five of the cutest pictures from the day before. She wrote a brief paragraph introducing her followers to the social media celebrity Sir Lancelot and tagging Kelvin Manor in the post. Within a few minutes, Bernie had liked and commented on the post and cross-posted it to her own account.

Then the likes started flooding in.

After ten minutes, the post had accumulated four

hundred likes – more than the Charmed account had attracted for any one post before. And still they kept coming. Bernie was right. Cute animals were a winner.

It was almost noon when Harper wandered over to Luna's desk with her phone in her hand.

"Hey, boss. You might find this interesting. I'm getting texts that there's some kind of scene happening in the covered market."

Luna looked up from her paperwork. "What kind of scene?"

"My cousin says the two mums of the dead guy are having a fight right in front of Granger's Organics."

"When you say the two moms ...?"

Harper consulted her phone. "The one is claiming to be his birth mother, while the other says she's his real mother. They're yelling at each other."

Luna saved her work and stood up. "I'd better go and check it out. Can we swap our lunch slots, Harper? I'll take lunch now and you take it at one o'clock."

"Sure, boss. Just make sure you remember all the juicy details to tell me when you get back."

Luna grabbed her coat and ran out of the store. She jogged along Beach Road wishing, not for the first time, that she were fitter.

She arrived at the entrance to the covered market, and speed walked towards Granger's Organics. The market smelled distractingly delicious – of cinnamon and fresh baking. Luna would have been able to locate the source of the ruckus even without Harper's directions because the ladies concerned were not bothering to keep their voices down.

A small knot of people had gathered in front of Ellie Granger's store. Luna spotted Tina Kitson standing next to her mother who was shouting at a woman of about the same age. That had to be Paul Robard's adoptive mother. Behind her stood two men. One was in his seventies like her, while the other looked to be about fifty. Luna guessed that they were her husband and son. The rest seemed to be random onlookers, including Ellie herself who stood at the entrance to her store, wringing her hands and trying to shoo everyone away.

Mrs. Robard appeared to be taking Mrs. Kitson to task over the fact that Paul's first set of adoptive parents had returned him to the agency.

"Four years!" she shouted. "That's how long he was with them before they decided that they actually didn't want to be parents after all. Can you imagine that happening to a four-year-old boy? Can you?"

"Of course I can imagine that. I raised a child of my own, you know." Mrs. Kitson indicated Tina. "But the point is that it had nothing to do with me. Every couple that applied to adopt our baby had been vetted by social services and by the agency. They picked the couple that they liked best."

"Well, they didn't do a very good job, did they?"

"How was I to know?"

"You could have kept track of him. You could have chosen to keep up with how he was doing. You would have known about those terrible years he spent in foster care."

"That's not what we were advised to do in those days. They told us that a closed adoption was best."

"Would you have chosen an open adoption if you'd been told to?" Mrs. Robard fired at her.

"Of course she would," said Tina, having apparently decided to side with her mother.

Mrs. Kitson shook her head. "Don't talk nonsense,

darling. We would have chosen not to keep up contact. We believed that was best for everyone concerned."

"You mean it was best for you!" yelled Mrs. Robard. "You couldn't wait to wash your hands of him."

"I believed I was making the best decision for him at the time."

"Why?" demanded Mrs. Robard. "Why did you give him up? Were you living in poverty? Were you a single mother in desperate circumstances? Were you unable to raise him?"

"It ... wasn't like that," said Mrs. Kitson. "It just wasn't the right time. My husband and I planned to have a baby a couple of years later, when I could stay home full time and look after it."

"Oh, it wasn't *exactly* the right time, was it? So, because it wasn't one hundred per cent *convenient* for you, you condemned him to rejection and misery and a lifetime of wandering why he wasn't good enough."

Luna noticed Ellie Granger beckoning to her. She skirted the combatants and joined Ellie in the doorway to Granger's Organics.

"Why do they have to yell at each other in front of my shop?" demanded Ellie. "They're scaring everyone away. I haven't had a customer in the shop since they started."

"They're certainly causing a scene."

"Can't you ... I don't know ... poof them away, or something?" Ellie clicked her fingers and blew on them as though magicking the ladies away.

Luna had to smile. "No, I can't *poof* them away. But perhaps I can persuade them to move along."

Mrs. Kitson was still shouting. "If I hadn't given him up, you would never have become his mother. Is that really what you would have wanted?"

"I would have wanted him to be happy. I would have wanted him not to have died."

Mrs. Kitson folded her arms across her chest. "Well, that had nothing to do with me."

"Are you sure? Where's your husband, Mrs. Kitson? I hear he's been missing for a while. I hear he has a grudge against Paul."

"Because the Paul *you* raised was trying to extort money from him. And my husband isn't missing. He is joining me here on the island later today. He has merely been away on business for a few days."

"I wonder where he was on the night Paul was killed," said Mrs. Robard. "I bet ferry records would be able to tell us a lot."

Mrs. Kitson took a deep breath. "I suppose you want to blame him for the break-in at the Scout Hall this morning too. When everyone knows that it's *your* older son who is the big hobby collector. I've heard he's very interested in jigsaw puzzles."

Mrs. Robard's eyes darted from left to right. This seemed to be the first she was hearing about the break-in. "If someone broke into the Scout Hall, they were probably trying to figure out what puzzle Paul tried to buy just before his death. That sounds like something your husband might be interested in."

Before Mrs. Kitson could answer, Luna stepped between them. It wouldn't be appropriate for her to touch either one of them, but she attempted to radiate as much calming energy as possible.

"I can tell you exactly what Paul tried to buy on the night he was killed." Luna raised her voice to make sure that everyone in the little gathering heard her. A sudden silence fell over the group.

"What does it matter what my brother was trying to buy?" asked the man, who looked to be about fifty. "You don't have to tell us that. He was always hunting around for some new bargain or other."

Luna swept the group with her eyes. "And I can tell you where it is too," she added.

This time no one objected.

"Really?" Tina's voice sounded strained. "You know where it is right now?"

Luna nodded. "I do. It is a vintage, hand-cut, five-thousand-piece jigsaw puzzle showing a scene from the Moonstone Village High Street from the nineteen-thirties."

Tina Kitson opened her mouth and then closed it again.

Luna looked around to see if anyone had anything to say. When the silence persisted, she continued.

"The puzzle is at Charmed Bookstore on Beach Road. You'll find it in the non-fiction section. It's about half built at the moment. Anyone is welcome to come in and spend a little time working on it. We just ask that you not remove or damage any pieces."

There was another silence. It was broken by the man Luna took to be Paul's adoptive father.

"That sounds like a valuable puzzle. Should you really leave it out in the open where anyone could get at it?"

"There's always someone in the bookstore," said Luna. "We keep an eye on it."

"Shouldn't the police take possession of it?" asked Tina.

"The police have already got all the evidence they need from it. They returned it to me because I bought it from Marcus Blackstone."

"Well," said Mrs. Robard. "I never understood Paul's attachment to all that hobby stuff."

"It was his job, Mum," said her son. "It wasn't something he just did for fun."

"I suppose that's true, but he enjoyed it too. I guess it was his way of comforting himself at a time when his life was very difficult." She glared at Mrs. Kitson.

Luna stepped in before the fight could resume. "I think we should all move along now. We're blocking the entrance to Granger's Organics and there's really no point in any more arguing."

For a moment, no one moved. Then they dispersed in their little family groups.

Ellie huffed out a sigh of relief. "At last. I thought they'd never leave. Thanks, Luna."

"You're very welcome."

"Before you go on your way, I have a couple of sick plants for you to take a look at, if you have time."

Luna checked her watch. "Sure. I need to be back by one so Harper can go on lunch, but I have a few minutes."

Ellie herded her into the shop. "I meant to show you yesterday when you were in here buying rue, but I was distracted by another customer. This pot of thyme looks a little sad, as you can see. And this fennel here is just about dead. And I don't suppose you could give me anything to keep my basil growing for longer, can you?"

Luna walked a slow circle around the afflicted plants. She dipped her forefinger into the soil of each one to get a feeling for what was amiss. Then she trailed her fingers through their leaves.

She turned to Ellie. "The thyme needs to be supplemented with bonemeal. And you could give it one extra watering per week. The basil is ready to go to seed. You need to stop nipping off the flowers when they appear and allow it to make seeds. Then store the seeds until spring and allow this plant to die. There is a natural growing season for all things that we should respect. The fennel will need special treatment at my place. I'll take it with me now and text you when you can come and pick it up."

"Yes, I thought it might be serious enough for hospital treatment. Thanks, Luna. You're the best."

Chapter 18

*L*una texted Melinda Knight as she walked back to the bookstore. She listed everyone who had been present at the altercation in the covered market and told Melinda exactly what she had said to them. She ended off with a comment that the hook was well and truly baited now and that it would be interesting to see who responded to the lure.

A minute later, Melinda responded with a row of thumbs-up emojis. Luna took that to mean that she approved of her course of action but was too busy to comment at length.

After another minute, Melinda responded with a message saying, *"Just be careful. You're a formidable opponent, but you're not bullet-proof."*

A shiver of foreboding touched Luna's spine. She was indeed not bullet-proof, and she had turned herself into a target for someone who had already committed murder once.

Luna didn't know for sure that the half-built puzzle in her bookstore was the murderer's target, but she strongly suspected that it was. The murderer might not know what the puzzle represented either but would probably be interested enough to find out.

She walked into Charmed just a minute before one o'clock.

"Thanks for swapping lunch shifts," she called to Harper. "You can go out now if you like."

Harper appeared with a backpack slung over one shoulder. "I do like. The bakery in the covered market is selling hot, fresh crêpes with lemon and cinnamon sugar right now. Shall I bring one back for you? Jim already said that he wants one."

"Sure. That sounds great. Take the money from petty cash. That must have been what smelled so good at the market."

"Will do. And as a bonus, I'll stop in at Granger's Organics and get all the gossip from Ellie. Speaking of which." She cut her eyes towards the non-fiction section and lowered her voice. "Look over there."

"Hmm." Luna saw a man working on the jigsaw puzzle. Pyewacket perched on the table next to him, keeping him under strict surveillance. He had his back to Luna, but there was something familiar about him.

"Anyway, I'll leave you to it." Harper headed out the door. "Don't ruin your appetite for the crêpe by eating something foolish like a salad."

Luna laughed and shook her head. Then she took a stroll over to the non-fiction section. She was simply going to say hello to her cat – a perfectly normal thing to do.

The man turned around at her approach. It was Paul Robard.

Luna was so startled that she almost staggered.

Then the rational part of her brain took over as she realized that she was looking at a much older man. Paul Robard had been forty-something, and this man was seventy at least. But the resemblance was uncanny. Luna had spent enough time looking at photos of Paul online to be very familiar with his face. The eyes, nose, and mouth were almost identical to this man. It was only in the shape of the eyebrows that their faces differed. That and the fact that this man looked like a version of Paul Robard that had been left out in the sun.

Luna had a good idea who she was looking at, but wanted it confirmed before she made any assumptions.

Plastering a friendly smile on her face, she stepped forward. "How are you getting on with the puzzle? Oh, I see you've made good progress."

He had completed another topiary bush that was in the shape of the letter R. He had also done some work on one of the shop fronts.

He frowned at Luna. "I would have made much better progress if this were the correct box for the puzzle. It's sheer carelessness to pack a puzzle in the wrong box."

"That's true, but many consider that to be part of the charm of this puzzle. It's similar enough to the image on the box that the box is a good guide, but there are little surprises in the puzzle itself – Easter eggs, if you will."

He snorted. "Easter eggs. What nonsense. It's an inconvenience, that's what it is."

Luna tutted. "I wouldn't take it too seriously. It's just a bit of fun to entertain the customers. I bought it at the jigsaw puzzle convention that is currently taking place in our Scout Hall in the High Street. It's not meant to be taken too seriously."

He made a humphing noise as he pawed through the pieces.

Luna's smile widened and she held out her hand. "I'm Luna Larkspur, by the way. This is my bookstore."

For a moment she thought he would refuse to shake hands with her. Then he clasped her hand with obvious reluctance and said, "Ivan Kitson."

"Oh, I think I've met your wife and daughter. They'll be so relieved to hear that you've arrived on the island. No one seemed to know where you were."

"More nonsense. I'm under no obligation to check in every single day. Besides, I just spoke to my wife on the phone. She was the one who tipped me off about this ..." He caught himself and continued smoothly. "She told me to be sure to visit your bookshop."

"Your visit to Moonstone Island is a sad one, I'm afraid. Please accept my condolences."

His frown deepened. "Condolences? I have no use for your condolences. I've suffered no loss that I'm aware of."

"Well, I mean, surely ... Paul Robard."

"An accident of biology, no more. You can't expect me to shed crocodile tears over a man I haven't laid eyes on since he was a grubby brat."

"He was trying to blackmail you, wasn't he?" said Luna.

It was his turn to look shocked. "What do you mean? Who told ...?" He stopped himself again.

"Your wife told everyone at dinner last night at the hotel. I can understand that you aren't shedding any tears over him. In fact, I would say it's quite convenient for you to have him out of the way."

Ivan Kitson swept her with a furious glance. "You, young lady, are unpardonably rude." Then he stormed out of the bookstore.

Luna mimed wiping sweat from her brow. "Phew. That's him gone."

It had begun to dawn on her that while she was using the puzzle as bait, she didn't want anyone to finish it except her.

She scratched the cat behind his ears. "I need to remove a few crucial pieces that will stop anyone from solving the secret of the puzzle. But which ones?"

Crouching low, Pyewacket sniffed the unplaced pieces. Then he swiped at them with his paw until he had separated five pieces from the rest.

"Those ones?" said Luna. "Are you sure?"

He sniffed the pieces again and used his paw to add one more to the little pile. Then he sat back with an attitude of finality.

"Excellent. Thank you, Pyewacket. I'll just pop these into my bag. Ouch!" She pulled back her hand as he dabbed at it with an annoyed paw. He hadn't actually hurt her, but he had startled her.

"What was that for?" Then it dawned on her. "Ohh. I'm not wearing my blocking cream, am I? Good thinking."

The bookstore had filled up with lunchtime browsers. One of them would surely have noticed if the puzzle pieces had started glowing.

Leaving the cat in charge of the puzzle, Luna went to apply her blocking cream.

～

Harper's return after lunch was heralded by a deliciously sweet and tangy smell. In each hand, she carried a large crêpe wrapped in wax paper.

"One for you." She handed a crepe to Jim. "And one for you." She handed the other to Luna. Then she went to resume her duties at the coffee station.

Jim brought his over to the non-fiction section to join Luna in staring at the mysterious puzzle.

She took a bite of her crêpe and closed her eyes in bliss. "Oh, my gosh. This is amazing. The crunchy cinnamon sugar, the bite of lemon, and not to mention the hot crêpe."

"I know," said Jim, swallowing his first mouthful. "Diane at the bakery does a marvelous job. You never know when she's going to do one of her pancake popups, but it's always worth waiting for."

"Oh, that's right," said Luna. "You guys call these pancakes, don't you? For me a pancake is a different thing. It's thicker and you pour syrup over it."

Jim nodded. "We'd call that a crumpet, or a flapjack. Although in Scotland, flapjack is an entirely different kind of baked good. It's made of toasted oats and cut into squares. What we English might call a crunchie."

Luna knew she would never remember the difference. And it didn't matter. The crêpe she was eating right now was delicious, and that was all that mattered.

"Who was that I saw working on the puzzle earlier?" asked Jim.

"That was Ivan Kitson – biological father to the late Paul Robard. They look shockingly alike."

"I thought he had gone missing?"

"Not according to him. Mind you, I wouldn't mind knowing exactly where he was on the night of the murder. Especially since Paul was allegedly trying to extort money out of him in return for not selling his adoption story to the media."

Jim frowned. "I can see how that might be a valid threat if any of them were celebrities, but why would the media care about this private family matter?"

"Agreed. It was a toothless threat, which is probably why

Kitson never agreed to it. But one can see how it could have led to bad blood between father and son."

"Indeed." Jim popped the last bite of his crêpe into his mouth and wiped his fingers on a napkin. His eyes remained on the puzzle. "B-A-R. I'm starting to get an idea of what the bushes will spell out in the end."

"You are?" said Luna. "What is it?"

He opened his mouth and then closed it again. "No. I don't want to send you down the wrong path if I'm mistaken. We need a few more letters to be sure. Do you mind if I do some work on it?"

"Please do. I've made sure that nobody can finish the puzzle by removing some crucial pieces. Pyewacket told me which ones."

Jim didn't blink. He stroked the cat until he purred. "Did he indeed? That was a wise move. If this puzzle is really the reason why Paul Robard lost his life, we can't treat it lightly."

"That's what I was thinking. By the way, I sent your mother a potted Rudbeckia to say thank you for dinner last night. They flower beautifully at this time of year."

"I know. She told me. She was delighted with it. Did you really grow it yourself?"

"Not from seed, but from a seedling. I thought it would be to her taste."

"You were right. She loves it. She wanted to know whether she should plant it out into the garden when she gets home or keep it in the pot?"

"It can stay in the container for another year. That way she can enjoy it in the house. After a year, it might need a bigger container or to be planted outside."

"I'll tell her," said Jim. "She really liked you, you know."

Luna laughed. "Let's rather say that she didn't completely hate me, which she was kind of expecting to do.

She's moving along the road toward liking me, but she's not there quite yet."

Jim's smile was wry. "You're far too intuitive for your own good. But she's my mum and I have the final say. She's further down the road to liking you than you might think."

Jim stood up and lobbed his balled-up napkin and wax paper into a garbage can. Then he placed a few pieces of the puzzle and Luna saw that the fourth topiary bush also spelled out the letter R.

"B-A-R-R," she mused.

Chapter 19

*D*eeply absorbed in puzzle-building, Luna let an hour of the afternoon slip away.

The next topiary bush eluded her, but she made progress on a couple of shopfronts – a hat shop for the well-dressed lady and a cheese shop that featured giant wheels of cheese in the window that made her feel quite hungry.

She was pulled out of this historical scene by her barista.

"Heads up, boss," said Harper. "I just sold another self-help book. There's almost nothing left of your display. You need to restock it, or to think of something else."

Leaving Pyewacket guarding the puzzle, Luna wandered over to the front desk. "Time to shift gears, I think. I want to ease into a seasonal display. We'll start off with some of our bloodiest horror novels on a backdrop of fall colors. Then we can mix it up with a display of non-fiction books about the paranormal."

Harper rubbed her hands together in glee. "Halloween's coming. What are we doing for it?"

"We'll slowly add decorations to the store in the days running up to the thirty-first. And then on the day, obviously, you and I will be dressed up. I thought I'd go as a witch."

Harper laughed and rolled her eyes. "Talk about type-casting."

Luna pretended she hadn't heard. "And you can go as whatever you want, including a witch."

"Ooh, I'll go as Jason from *Friday the Thirteenth*. I just need to find an ice-hockey mask."

"When I said you can go as whatever you like," Luna continued. "I meant something cute and fun that will entertain the small children I am hoping to attract to the store. Not something terrifying that will give them nightmares for months. I, for example, will go as a nice, friendly witch, not a scary one."

Harper pouted. "Sure, boss. Whatever. I'll save the hockey mask for going out with my friends on Halloween night."

"Perfect."

"Okay, but can I go shopping for the decorations? Please. I really want to do it. Can I? Huh? Can I? Please, please, please ..."

Luna blocked her ears. "Yes! Yes, you can go shopping for the decorations."

Harper did a happy dance. "Yay! What's my budget?"

"Um, I don't know. A hundred pounds?"

"Nah, that's too much. Fifty will be fine. I can make this place look like Dracula's castle for fifty pounds."

"Go nuts," recommended Luna. "But remember – spooky and fun rather than nightmarish and terrifying. We'll lure the kids in with a pumpkin carving competition and prizes for dressing up and then sell books and merchandise to their parents."

"Sneaky," said Harper. "I like it." She looked up as something caught her eye. "Don't look now, but your puzzle has attracted yet another would-be builder. I told you not to look!"

"Hush," said Luna. "He's not looking at us. I recognize him from the fight outside Granger's Organics. That's Ellis Robard – Paul Robard's adoptive brother. He has also spent time in the hobby business."

Harper noticed a customer appearing at the serving hatch. "Go get 'em tiger." She hurried off to take the coffee order.

Luna stayed where she was for a moment, watching her quarry. He attempted to place several pieces of the puzzle, but couldn't seem to make them fit. A shade of annoyance crossed his face. In a sudden movement, he scooped up the cat and deposited him on the floor.

Pyewacket promptly jumped back up on the table again and resumed his post. The man picked him up once more and put him on the floor. And once again the cat jumped back up onto the table.

As the man reached for him again, Luna hurried forward. Pyewacket was one millisecond away from administering a sharp swat to the man. But Jim got there before her.

Luna couldn't hear what he was saying, but she saw the way he stroked Pyewacket to sooth him and angled his body to block the man's access to the cat. It was at times like these that Luna realized that Jim was really rather tall and broad-shouldered compared with other men, for all his slightly nerdy, academic demeanor.

The man made an impatient gesture, but Jim didn't budge.

"Hello," said Luna, putting on a bright smile and a ditzy manner. "Everything all right here?"

"Not exactly," said Ellis Robard. "I'm allergic to cats and this man won't let me remove the animal from the table."

Luna opened her eyes wide. "But it's his table."

Ellis laughed. "It's his table? This table belongs to a cat?"

"That's right. That's his table and those are his chairs and over there are his books, and that's his coffee machine too."

"So, you're telling me this entire bookstore belongs to the cat?"

"He lives here, and so do I. Everything you see belongs to the two of us."

Ellis sighed. "All I want to do is try my hand at this puzzle. If it's all the same to you, I'd like to do it without itchy, streaming eyes and a stuffy nose. Is that too much to ask?"

Luna stared at his face. There wasn't a hint of redness about his eyes. "Take a pill. I can offer you one, if you like. But the cat isn't going anywhere."

"Fine, fine." He picked up another piece and tried to place it without success. He made a frustrated noise.

"This is so difficult. The fact that the box doesn't match the puzzle is a total nightmare. They shouldn't sell puzzles in this condition. The retailer should be held responsible."

"May I?" Jim removed the puzzle piece from Ellis's hand and placed it where it belonged – in the top right-hand quadrant of the cheese shop.

Ellis looked impressed. "Oh, you're good at this. Do another one."

Jim picked up a handful of pieces, glanced at the box, and began to place them in fairly quick succession. He was indeed good at this - much better than Luna, even now that she was getting the hang of puzzling. And he was considerably better than Ellis Robard who was surprisingly incompetent for one who had an interest in hobbies.

Luna noticed that Jim stayed away from the topiary bushes, concentrating on filling out the rest of the world of 1938 Moonstone Island.

The topiary bushes had, however, caught Ellis's eye. "Look at that. Those bushes have been trimmed into the shape of letters. B-A-R-R. Barr. What do you suppose that means?"

"I'm fairly sure it refers to a solicitor's office that was headquartered in the High Street back in the 1930s," said Jim. "Barr and Sons. They were a general solicitor's firm with a particular interest in patent law. Anyone who had created a new product or invention would apply for a patent through them."

"Is that so?" Ellis pulled out his phone and snapped a picture of the half-built puzzle. "Do they still exist, this firm of solicitors?"

"Indeed, they do. But they're not on the High Street anymore. I'm not sure where they moved to."

Ellis watched in fascination as Jim placed more pieces of the puzzle.

"I saw you in the covered market earlier," said Luna. "You're part of the Robard family, aren't you? You must be here for the funeral of the man who was killed a few days ago."

"Yes, Paul was my brother. My parents adopted him when I was thirteen years old. He must have been about eight at that stage."

"What was he like as a boy?"

Ellis's expression softened. "He was a dear little chap. So eager to please and so afraid to hope that this really was his final home. It took a long time for him to trust that we weren't going to return him to the foster care system like other families had."

Luna gave a sympathetic nod. "He was already interested in hobbies by then, wasn't he?"

"Very much so. He loved yo-yos and Rubik's cubes and green slime. He knew how to make slime from household ingredients. One of the first things we did together as brothers was to make our own slime and color it green. We sold it to kids at school and made a tidy profit."

"So, he got you interested in hobbies, rather than the other way round?"

"That's right. I caught the bug from him. And being older, I could pursue it further."

"Did you ever work in the hobby business?" asked Luna.

"As soon as I was able. The moment I turned sixteen, I got a weekend job working at Blackstone's Hobby Shop in Leeds. Paul was terribly jealous, of course, but he got his turn later on."

"What was Marcus Blackstone like to work for?"

Ellis looked surprised. "Oh, you know him?"

"Not really, but I bought this puzzle from him, and we chatted for a while."

"Well, he was a fair enough boss. Never unreasonable. But secretive, very secretive."

"Secretive about what?" asked Jim.

"He was always on the hunt for some new collector's item or other that would make his fortune. But he acted like everything was top secret. As though we, his staff, were going to try to steal away his latest find. I mean, he was the boss. Anything Blackstone's Hobby Shop acquired automatically belonged to him. It wasn't as though we could afford to undercut him. We were all broke. We could have helped him find whatever he was looking for if only he had been candid about it."

"Did he make any great finds over the years?" asked Luna.

"Now and then. He would go to local auctions and come back with limited-edition action figures or puzzles or comic books. I remember an old *Beano* annual that was worth rather a lot."

Jim smiled. "I loved the Beano books when I was a child."

"Really? You look a bit young for those, if you don't mind my saying."

"I raided my late father's collection. I think some of them even belonged to my grandfather. I read them over and over until they fell to bits."

Ellis's face twitched. "They were probably worth thousands of pounds. They should have been behind glass, not given to a small boy to destroy."

"I prefer to think that my mother gave them to me to enjoy. Is that what you believe – that games and hobbies should be behind glass rather than given to children to enjoy?"

The irritated look was back on Ellis's face. "It doesn't have to be one or the other. In every release of a new hobby item, some should be sold to the general public for ordinary use, and some should be kept aside for posterity."

"Fair enough," said Jim. "So did Marcus Blackstone never find a really big-ticket item?"

"Not as far as I know." Ellis indicated the puzzle Jim was working on. "Take this for example. It's an extremely rare, vintage, hand-cut puzzle with a uniqueness factor. What did you pay for it, if you don't mind my asking?"

"Two hundred and eighty pounds," said Luna.

"You see? That's very expensive for a jigsaw puzzle, but it's not a life-changing amount of money. I suspect Marcus is still in search of his life-changing item."

Ellis looked up as the front door chime sounded. The annoyance on his face deepened. "Mother."

Chapter 20

*M*rs. Robard entered the bookstore like a woman on a mission.

She turned sharp left and ordered a coffee from Harper. With that in hand, she began to browse the new releases section.

It seemed to Luna that she was deliberately making her way towards the puzzle.

Putting back a book she had been looking at, she glanced up and caught sight of her son for the first time. The expression that flickered across her face was unmistakable. She was as displeased to see him as he was to see her.

Smoothing out her expression, she walked towards them.

"Ellis."

"Mother."

She wagged a playful finger at him. "I thought I told you not to come here this afternoon. Whatever your poor brother was chasing before he died, it's not our business to try to make sense of it."

Ellis's lips tightened. "As I recall, the agreement was that none of us would come here this afternoon. In other words, you have no more business being here than I do."

She held her cup aloft. "I simply came in to get a coffee and to look for something to read."

Ellis frowned. "I find that hard to believe, Mother. While I know all about your caffeine addiction, it's news to me that you are much of a reader."

"Nonsense, dear. I frequently have a novel on the go."

"Be that as it may, I remain convinced that you came here to ferret out what you could about Paul's death."

"I'm his mother!"

"And I'm his brother. What's more, we were in the same line of business. But that didn't stop you from trying to discourage me from coming in here today."

Mrs. Robard's eyes were irresistibly drawn to the puzzle. She seemed to be hardly paying attention to what her son was saying.

"Is that it?" she demanded.

"Yes," said Luna. "That's the puzzle Paul tried to buy shortly before his death. No one knows why yet."

Mrs. Robard's attention was fixed on the puzzle. Almost as though she couldn't help herself, she too pulled out her phone and snapped a picture of it.

"B-A-R-R," she said. "What does that mean?"

When her son said nothing, Jim spoke up. "We think it's a reference to Barr and Sons – an old solicitors' firm that used to have its headquarters in the High Street. It has since moved, I believe."

Jim sent Luna a ghost of a wink, which she wasn't sure how to interpret.

"Barr and Sons," said Mrs. Robard. "Interesting. Why is the puzzle different to the image on the box?"

"No one knows that either," said Luna. "All we know is that Paul wanted this particular puzzle and no other."

Mrs. Robard's eyes filled with tears. "How I wish he had never gone into that stupid hobby business. You should never have led him down that road, Ellis. You were the one person he trusted."

Her son's frown deepened. "First of all, it was Paul who introduced me to his love for hobbies, not the other way round. And second, it's not as though I was leading him into a life of drugs or crime. The hobby business is harmless."

"My son is dead, so it can't be all that harmless."

"We don't know for sure that his death was connected to ..."

Mrs. Robard shouted him down. "Oh, nonsense, Ellis. That's not true and you know it. If Paul hadn't got involved in that world, he would still be alive today. That man, Marcus Blackstone, taught him to become obsessed with chasing collectors' items. And you can't deny that *you* introduced him to Paul because you did. You worked at that shop in Leeds first and Paul followed your lead."

"How was I to know what would happen? Paul was grateful to me for getting him the job at Blackstone's. Even you and Dad were pleased."

"He was never the same afterwards. The obsession took over his life. Like his preoccupation with that stupid comic book."

Ellis rolled his eyes. "We should get back to the B&B, Mother. These people can't possibly be interested in our squabbles."

"What comic book was that?" asked Luna.

"That stupid *Superman #1* or whatever it was. And first editions of the Biggles novels. Not to mention his ridiculous pursuit of those comics set in New Zealand. What were they called, Ellis? You know the ones. They were set on a sheep station."

When her son didn't answer, she sharpened her tone. "What were they called, Ellis?"

"*Footrot Flats*," Ellis said reluctantly.

"*Footrot Flats*! That's it. Even the name is ridiculous, but you would have sworn they represented the holy grail the way Paul went on about them."

Ellis looked at his watch. "We really should go now, Mother. Father will be wondering where we are."

"Oh, very well." She raised her hand in a gesture of farewell and allowed herself to be led away.

~

Luna and Jim looked at each other.

"I feel as though we just received some important information," said Luna. "But it's difficult to separate the wheat from the chaff in that conversation."

Jim typed something into his phone. "I'm making a note of those collector's items she mentioned. I'll text them to you. *Superman 1*, *Biggles* first editions, and *Footrot Flats*."

"Thanks. What was up with Barr and Sons? Is that a genuine firm of solicitors?"

Jim smiled. "It is, as it happens. But they never had their headquarters in the High Street, as far as I know. I've sent the Robards on a wild goose chase while we figure out what these topiary bushes really spell."

There was a pause of several minutes as he worked on the next section of the puzzle.

"It's an 'i'."

"An eye?" said Luna whose attention had wandered. "Oh, you mean the letter."

She looked at the puzzle and saw that the next tree in line was indeed trimmed into the shape of a lower-case i.

"B-a-r-r-i," said Luna. "What does it mean?"

Jim looked excited. "It means I was right. Probably. I began to suspect it when we had the first three letters. Now I'm almost certain."

"Certain of what?"

"That the bushes will spell out the word 'Barrington's'. It was a men's department store that occupied part of the High Street for decades. I think they went out of business in the 1940s. They sold everything the well-dressed gentleman needed – hats, scarves, gloves, shirts, suits, shoes. You name it. There was even a tobacconist on the premises, and a shoeshine stand. It was supposed to be a one-stop shop for men."

Luna looked at the image on the box. "Yes, I see the store here, tucked into a corner. It wasn't very big, was it?"

"The street level store front was small, but I believe they occupied the whole upper level of the building at one stage."

"So, both the image on the box and the image on the puzzle include Barrington's as one of the store fronts. But the image on the puzzle has the trees most likely spelling out the word Barrington's as though to draw one's attention to the department store. But why? What does it all mean?"

Jim stared at the puzzle. "Let's assume it has something to do with a collector's item that Paul Robard may have been aware of."

"Okay," said Luna. "But did he believe that this puzzle contained a clue about where to find the collector's item? Is that why he was so keen to get hold of it just before he died?" She paused in thought. "When was this puzzle made anyway?"

Jim picked up the box and turned it over in his hands, looking for a date. "Here it is. According to the box, the puzzle was made in 1973."

"So, what we have is a hand-made, limited-edition puzzle made in 1973 with a box that shows a street scene from the 1920s but a puzzle that shows a street scene from the late 1930s. And now in the twenty-first-century we have a man who may or may not have been killed for this puzzle."

"And all for the sake of a collector's item that probably dates from a different era altogether," said Jim.

"Speaking of which, I want to research those items that Paul's mother mentioned."

"Good idea." Jim dismantled the topiary bush he had just built – the one showing the letter 'i'. He handed the pieces to Luna. "Keep those with the other pieces you removed. We don't want anyone else to have Barrington's in mind just yet."

As Luna's fingers closed around the puzzle pieces, they began to glow. She almost dropped them.

"Whoa," said Jim. "That never gets old."

She rolled her eyes. "My blocking cream must be wearing off. I'd better reapply it."

"And I should get back to work," said Jim. "Although this is much more fun."

As he made his way back to the permanent collection, Luna called after him, "One last thing. How many people on the island today would remember the name Barrington's?"

He rubbed a hand over his chin. "Maybe the older generation. But it closed down nearly eighty years ago. I can't imagine there are many who still remember it. But there will be those who remember their parents mentioning it. I only know about it from my work as a cultural historian. As far as I know, the name didn't survive in any other form after the department store closed down. It wasn't even a family name. The people who owned it had a different last name. I can't think what it is right now, but I'll let you know when I find it."

Jim returned to his laptop and became absorbed in his work.

Luna decided to follow his example. Much as she itched to continue her research into Paul Robard's death, the bookstore came first. Harper had told her that the display window was looking depleted. It was time to perk it up and get some pre-Halloween interest going. She counted off dates on her fingers and discovered that there were five days left, up to and including Halloween. She would aim to create a different display for each day. She had been thinking about it and refining her original idea.

On Halloween itself, she decided, she would create a display of spooky children's books to lure families into the store. And on another day, she could have a display of thriller or horror novels that had been turned into movies. There were lots of those. But for today, she would go old school with the master of horror himself, Stephen King. She knew she had plenty of stock of his books, having catalogued authors with surnames beginning with K just recently.

The problem was that they were spread all over the store. Luna's late grandfather had used a shelving system that could only be described as erratic. Some Stephen King novels were shelved under Horror, some under Thriller and others under Contemporary. And the alphabetic system in each section was anything but reliable.

It was like a treasure hunt, ferreting them out of various corners of the store. Fortunately, Stephen King was a prolific writer and there was plenty of stock to choose from. Luna focused on his classic horror novels like *Carrie, Cujo, Salem's Lot, It, The Shining, and Misery.* Those would form the most prominent part of the display.

Luna's copies of *Carrie* ranged from threadbare paperbacks with torn covers and missing pages to some nearly new editions, and everything in between. For her window displays, she always tried to feature books in the best condition. Once those were sold out, customers could move onto the scruffier second or third-hand copies if they wanted to.

Humming happily to herself, Luna searched the attic for some suitably spooky props for her display.

Chapter 21

*T*he result was one of her finest efforts, if she did say so herself.

The window display was draped with orange and red scarves and decorated with plastic Jack O'Lanterns that would light up at night. She had sent Harper up the road to the party store for some cobwebs and bats that she could arrange and stick up around the books.

The display of classic Stephen King novels should prove irresistible to the aficionado and the first-time buyer alike. Luckily, the master of horror always had excellent cover designs.

Luna stepped outside to see what her display looked like from the street, which was the only perspective that really mattered.

A moment later, Harper joined her. "Looking good, boss. That should bring the punters in. Maybe a couple of artificial spiders clinging to those cobwebs?"

"I like it," said Luna.

"Then I'll pick some up on my way home this evening and we can place them tomorrow morning."

"Perfect."

Feeling as though she had done her part to stimulate sales, Luna settled at the front desk and began Googling the collectors' items Mrs. Robard had mentioned. Her first search was for the Biggles books because the name had stuck in her mind, and she had not heard of them before.

It turned out that Biggles was the name of a character in a series of British children's books from the 1930s. An ace World War One pilot, Biggles' earliest appearance was in a short story. The first full-length novel featuring the character was called *Biggles of the Camel Squadron.* It had been published in 1934 and there were several vendors on the internet claiming to have first editions for sale. The prices of these seemed to range widely according to the condition of the book. The most expensive copy Luna could find was offered for three thousand dollars.

Once again, she was left wondering about the price of a human life. Three thousand dollars didn't seem to be what Ellis Robard had referred to as a 'life-changing' amount of money, but money meant different things to different people.

Throughout history, humans had been killed for what one person might regard as a trivial amount of money, but that another might desperately seek. Indeed, people had been killed simply for being in the wrong place at the wrong time.

It was impossible to know what might drive someone to take the life of another. Three thousand dollars wasn't as much as Luna expected, but she put the possibility on the backburner and moved on to the next item.

The *Footrot Flats* series of comic strips turned out to have been written by the New Zealand cartoonist Murray Ball. The comic strips were first collected into book form in 1978.

A first edition of that was offered in good condition on Amazon for fifty US dollars.

If three thousand dollars wasn't convincing enough as a motive for murder, fifty dollars really fell short.

Fully intending to move on, Luna nevertheless found herself falling down an internet rabbit hole into the world of Murray Ball's *Footrot Flats*. The cartoons were delightfully addictive, and before she knew it, she had ordered two complete sets of the collections to stock her shelves with. The fact that she would read them first before putting them out for the customers was neither here nor there.

Tearing herself away from the adventures of Wal and the Dog, she moved on to the final collector's item.

Mrs. Robard had said something about *Superman 1*. The internet informed Luna that *Superman #1* had first appeared in 1939 and was considered a collector's item of high value. The price it would fetch at auction depended on the condition of the comic book and whether it had been restored or not. Recent sales of the comic book ranged from between two hundred thousand dollars and four hundred thousand dollars.

"Now *that* is more like it," she muttered.

For most people that would indeed be regarded as a life-changing sum of money.

Luna wasn't sure why she didn't feel more excited at the discovery.

Perhaps it was because every time she started a new search, Google asked her whether she didn't mean *Action Comics #1*. Instead of ignoring that result, she clicked on it and discovered something that made her sit up straight.

The first appearance of the character Superman in comic book form was not in *Superman #1* at all. He had first appeared in *Action Comics #1* in 1938.

Just reading the date gave Luna tingles.

The all-American superhero in his patriotic blue and red costume had been created at the beginning of the Second World War, years before America ever joined the conflict.

Most striking of all was the fact that the last time a copy of *Action Comics #1* had gone to auction, it had sold for 3.25 million dollars.

It was, quite simply, the most valuable collector's item in the world.

Of course, Mrs. Robard hadn't said anything about *Action Comics*. She had mentioned *Superman #1*. But perhaps she simply knew as little about such matters as Luna herself and had got the two confused.

"How are you getting on?" asked Jim as he passed Luna's desk on his way back from getting coffee.

"Have a look at this." She spread out her notes for him to look at. It didn't take long. His ability to read a situation at a glance was always impressive.

"You've decided that *Biggles* and *Footrot Flats* are non-starters because there's not enough money at stake?"

Luna nodded. "I mean, who really knows? But, yes."

"These sums of money look more convincing." Jim tapped Luna's notes. "A few hundred thousand dollars is a large amount in anyone's book, but 3.25 million dollars is crazy money."

"Enough to make someone do crazy things?" said Luna.

"Definitely."

She sat back and sighed. "How likely is it, though? *Action Comics #1* was released in America in 1938. Two hundred thousand copies were printed. What are the chances that one of those found its way across the Atlantic and all the way to Moonstone Island just as Britain went to war against

Germany? And what are the chances that anyone truly believes that one of those first edition comics survived into the twenty-first century?"

"Or that an unusual hand-cut puzzle contains a clue as to its whereabouts?" added Jim. "I agree, it's not a likely scenario. But it would certainly explain why Paul Robard met his death at a jigsaw puzzle convention two days ago. Of course, that doesn't get us any closer to figuring out who killed him."

"If we're right about the motive," said Luna. "Then it must have been someone who knew what Paul was on the trail of and believed that he was getting close to finding it. Someone in the hobby business, perhaps. Or a friend or relative he told about his quest."

"You think he was betrayed by someone he trusted?"

"Quite possibly. After all, that was what had happened to him his whole life long."

~

By five o'clock, Luna was alone in the shop with the cat as her only companion.

Harper had skipped off for a night out with her friends, while Jim had gone to get ready for dinner at the hotel with his mother, his sister, and Viola. It wasn't clear why the Cooke ladies had extended their stay on the island for yet another night, but Luna presumed it had something to do with wedding shopping.

She popped outside to check on her window display. A few books had already been sold, so she filled it out with more offerings from Charmed's Stephen King collection. Then she stepped onto the sidewalk again to confirm that her display was symmetrical and pleasing to the eye. Satisfied, she unhooked the front door and went inside, preparing to close the door behind her.

The door was wrenched out of her hands, and she was shoved violently forwards.

As Luna staggered and tried to regain her footing, she heard the door slam shut behind her and a lock click into place. The next moment, the store was plunged into gloom as the electric light flicked off.

She spun around in alarm, her heart nearly beating out of her chest. She gasped when the shadowy figure stepped closer, and she saw that it was Ivan Kitson.

"What are you doing in my store?" she demanded. "Get out immediately."

"Not until you tell me why you are spreading a story around the island that I killed my biological son."

Luna breathed in slowly, trying to calm her nerves. "I have not said anything of the sort to anybody."

"Then why did the police call me in for questioning this afternoon? You admitted that you're friendly with that woman detective, whatever her name is. Where else would the story have come from?"

"From any number of sources," said Luna. "It was your wife who told everyone that Paul Robard tried to blackmail you before his death. You confirmed it yourself this afternoon. It's only natural that the police would want to speak to you about that." Luna was trapped between him and her desk. She tried to shuffle sideways, but he boxed her in.

"Keep still. That squalling brat was not supposed to bother us again. He was gone from our lives. The fact that he has come back to haunt us even after his death is thanks to your meddling."

Ivan Kitson might have been over seventy, but he was an intimidating figure of a man.

"What meddling? If you want to be mad at someone, be mad at your wife. She's the one who goes around telling everyone your business."

A ripple of irritation seemed to go through his body. A flutter of movement caught Luna's eye and she saw something fall from his jacket pocket onto the floor.

"Stop talking about my wife. My family and I take care of each other. You interfered by buying that jigsaw puzzle and setting it up in here. What did you think was going to happen?"

"I thought it would provoke some interesting reactions," said Luna. "I guess I was right about that." Keeping an eye on him, she knelt to pick up the piece of paper that had fallen from his coat. The shape and color of it looked familiar. "Looks like you dropped something."

He glanced at the ground. Luna took advantage of his inattention to side-step him so that he no longer stood between her and the front door. She glanced at the piece of paper. It was, as she suspected, a ticket for the Moonstone Island ferry. But the most interesting thing about it was the date.

She held it out to him. "Is this yours?"

He snatched it from her hand and shoved it into his pocket. "Yes, it's mine. So what?"

"So, it proves that you travelled from Brighton to Moonstone Island on the afternoon ferry three days ago. Just in time for the jigsaw puzzle convention. You told the police you were not on the island on the night your biological son was killed. This suggests otherwise."

"Listen ..." He lunged forward and grabbed Luna's wrist with unforgiving strength.

"Let go of me." Luna's adrenalin spiked, her anger rose,

and her body did what it always did when someone laid hostile hands on her.

Ivan released her and stumbled backwards, shaking his hand as though someone had held it to a flame.

At that moment, Pyewacket darted forward and sank his fangs into the man's ankle. Luna heard the faint popping sound his teeth made as they punctured the skin.

The man gasped and staggered towards the door. He fumbled with the lock, whimpering as his blistered hand made contact. Then he flung the door open and escaped into the street.

Luna crouched down to stroke the cat. She held up her right hand. "High five. We tag-teamed him."

The cat reared up and bumped her hand with his head.

"Close enough."

Chapter 22

*B*oth cat and owner remained agitated throughout the evening.

Pyewacket wouldn't let Luna out of his sight, as though he were afraid she would get into trouble if he took his eyes off her for a moment.

Equally concerned was Melinda Knight when Luna texted her the story. No sooner had Luna pressed SEND on her text than the phone rang. Her friend was clearly a speed reader.

"He put his hands on you?" Melinda said in response to Luna's 'Hello.'

"Well, he grabbed me and shoved me and locked me inside with him."

"That's illegal."

"Yeah, I got that part. But he's gone now. Pyewacket bit him, and I ... well ... I burned him a bit."

"You burned ..." Melinda sighed. Luna couldn't almost hear the gears in her head turning over. "Never mind. I don't want to know about that part. The main thing is that you're safe and Pyewacket is a hero."

"He's sitting here staring at me right now. Equal parts concern and disapproval, I'd say."

"I know how he feels. You should press charges."

"Against my cat?"

Another sigh. "Against your assailant, Luna. Against Ivan Kitson. He assaulted you and trespassed on your property."

"Urrgh. Do I have to?"

"You don't have to do anything. But remember, if he did it to you, he is probably doing it to others too."

"Yes, that's true." All Luna wanted to do was have dinner and an early night, but Melinda had made a good point. If he had done it to her, he would do it to others. "But there were no witnesses. It's my word against his."

"Witnesses aren't necessary. You just have to be steady and consistent in your story."

"Plus, he has burn marks on his hands. What if he turns around and accuses *me* of assault?"

Melinda was silent for a moment. "I'll tell you what. You don't have to go as far as pressing charges if you don't want to. You could just file a report against him."

"How do I do that?"

"Email me a full statement of what happened, and I'll do the paperwork. I'll bring it around for you to sign in the morning. Then it will all be on record, and you can decide later if you want to take it any further."

"Okay, I can do that."

"Good." Melinda sounded pleased. "I hate to think of him getting off scot-free."

Pyewacket tapped Luna with a paw, as though to remind her of something. Then it hit her.

"Oh, I nearly forgot. He had a ferry ticket in his pocket."

"Who did? Ivan Kitson?"

"Yes, it fell out while he was yelling at me. It proves that he arrived on the island on the day Paul Robard was murdered."

"Really? Because according to him he was off on a business trip somewhere."

"Seems he was lying about that." Luna sat back and closed her eyes.

"Do you still have it?" Melinda asked.

"No. He snatched it out of my hand when I confronted him with it. But I got a good look at it. It was issued in his name for the late-afternoon ferry."

"Then there'll be someone who remembers seeing him on board. I'll check it out, thanks. It's not like he doesn't have motive."

"Yes, his biological son was trying to blackmail him - threatening to tell the world how Kitson abandoned him unless he paid him not to."

"And we now know that he's a violent and impulsive man."

"Hmm."

"Why don't you sound more excited?" asked Melinda. "It's a strong lead."

"I'd like to know more about what Robard did on that last day. Who did he speak to? Where did he go?"

"So would I, but we've already spoken to his biological sister, Tina, and his former employer, Marcus Blackstone, who hardly seems to remember him. I'm not sure that anyone else was aware of his presence."

"I know. But I wonder if they have really told us all they know."

"Well, if you want to speak to them again, knock yourself out. Just let me know if you learn anything interesting."

~

As she often did in the evening, Luna took refuge in baking. She hadn't made her oatmeal and raisin cookies in a while, so she opened the *Larkspur Family Recipe Book* on the correct page and began to gather her ingredients. The recipe was called *Oatmeal and Raisin Biscuits to Aid Digestion and Promote Regularity*. The first time Luna had made them, there had been an outbreak of diarrhea on the island. Then she had cut back on the saltpeter the recipe called for and the second time had passed without incident.

Harper had been skeptical about whether the cookies would sell on a second occasion, but the islanders had proved her wrong. Apparently, the cookies were irresistibly delicious, even with the threat of severe indigestion in your future.

Luna had assembled almost all her ingredients when she realized she was short of raisins. She barely had enough for eighteen cookies and not nearly enough for thirty-six. She would pop to the Kwikmart for more.

It was after six pm, but she was confident of finding the grocery store still open. Its hours were erratic but even if it were closed with all the lights off you could usually ring the doorbell to the apartment above the store and find a Brave family member willing to open up for you in an emergency. Luna knew that her raisin shortage would qualify as an emergency in the eyes of Harper's family.

The nights were drawing in on Moonstone Island as October came to a close. And when the clocks went back on the twenty-ninth it would be even more dramatic. Most of the stores on Beach Road had shut for the day. Only the pier that extended into the sea like a long and cheerful finger was still in full swing. It was the one part of the island that never closed. At three o'clock in the morning you could still see the lights twinkling and hear the buzz and squeaks of the slot machines.

It was the engine that kept the island's economy going – attracting tourists to the village all year round. Luna wished it didn't have to exist, but knew that she and others bene-fitted from it.

Brave's Kwikmart was very much open. It bustled with customers who had popped in on their way home from work. One of Harper's older sisters manned the cash register while her mother stood hipshot near the freezers listening to a customer and old friend complain about the full moon that had kept her awake the night before.

"Like a bleeding searchlight it was, Vera," the woman said. "Shining into me bedroom, bright enough to read by. And this at two o'clock in the bleeding morning."

"You say this was last night, Marge?" asked Harper's mom sympathetically.

"This is what I'm telling you, Vera. Last night, it was. Not last week. Not last month. It was last night. And that's why I've been so bleeding tired the whole day today."

"I only ask because it's not full moon at the moment, Marge. Not by a long shot." Harper's mom looked up and caught sight of Luna edging past with a bag of raisins in her hand. "Look at that, that's our Luna, so it is. She's Red Ricky's granddaughter. She'll know."

Vera Brave extended a beringed hand and clutched at Luna's sleeve.

"A moment of your time, Luna."

"What can I do for you ladies?"

"What's up with the moon these days? It's not full yet, is it?"

Luna had no idea why she always knew the exact phase

of the moon without having to look it up, but she did. She couldn't remember a time when she hadn't known it. And apparently her grandfather had been the same.

"Waxing crescent," she replied automatically. "It'll only be full on the twelfth of November."

"There you go, Marge," said Vera. "It can't possibly have been the full moon that woke you. It's not even half full yet. It must have been a light from one of the neighbors."

An untrusting soul, Marge pulled out her phone and double-checked Luna's information. "Full moon on the twelfth of November," she read. "You're right. But that wasn't no electric light, I saw. Why, it couldn't possibly have been."

Her interest piqued, Luna interrupted her journey to the cash register to join the ladies in blocking the freezer aisle.

"What exactly did you see, if I may ask?"

"A jolly great yellowish light that made my bedroom too bright for anyone to sleep in. Woke me up from a lovely dream about Clint Eastwood, so it did."

Vera rubbed her arm sympathetically. "That's hard luck, Marge. What did Fred say?"

"Slept through the whole thing, the lucky so-and-so."

"Did you look out the window to see where the light was coming from?" asked Luna.

Marge snorted. "I did not. Why would I when I thought it was the moon? The moon's in the sky, see. You don't need to check where the moon is."

Luna had to concede that this was true. She tried a different approach. "Which way do your bedroom windows face? Perhaps we can figure out where the light was coming from."

"They face north-west, love. We're on the High Street, just above the building society. We get a sea view and lots of lovely light in the afternoon. That's when you *want* the light, innit, Vera? Not at two o'clock in the bleeding morning. Next you'll be telling me it wasn't the moon at all, but the sun."

Harper's mom shrugged. "Not me, Marge. I haven't the faintest clue what it might have been."

"And what about the bleeding humming?"

"Humming?" asked Luna. This was the first she had heard about any humming.

"Marge here was telling me that the light was accompanied by a kind of humming sound," said Vera.

"Humming or vibrating," Marge clarified. "You could describe it either way."

"How long did it last?"

"Just a few minutes, but it was bothersome enough for me to lie awake for ages afterwards. And the bleeding light didn't go away for an hour or more. Is it any wonder I'm exhausted today?"

"It's a shame, that's what it is," said Vera.

Both ladies looked at Luna as though expecting her to produce a coherent explanation for these phenomena.

Her mystified shrug seemed to irritate them.

"You can do better than that, love," said Vera. "You being Red Ricky's granddaughter and all."

Luna opened her mouth to ask what that had to do with anything, but closed it again. If she didn't want to hear what the islanders thought of her and her probable connection to anything weird that might be going on, she shouldn't ask for it.

"Tell you what, I'll take a stroll up to the High Street right now to check it out. If anything unusual is going on, perhaps I'll spot it."

The ladies beamed at her. They approved of this proactive attitude.

"Just let me pay for my baked beans, love," said Marge.

"And I'll come with you. I'll show you exactly where the light was coming from."

So, Luna paid for her raisins and Marge paid for the baked beans that she said she planned to warm up in a saucepan and put on toast for her husband's 'tea'. It had taken Luna a while to get used to hearing the evening meal described as 'tea'. 'Tea' evoked images of a slice of cake and a cup of Tetley's. But many people used it to refer to the last savory meal of the day, often eaten as early as five or six pm. That was something Luna would refer to as dinner or supper.

Then she had discovered that not all British people used the same terms. Jim and his family, for example, used the words 'breakfast', 'lunch', 'afternoon tea', and 'dinner' the same way she did. So perhaps it was a regional thing.

∾

"How's business, love?" Marge asked as they tackled the steep road up to the High Street. "Better than in your grand-dad's time, I hope? You know, I never understood how that man made a living, not even when your grandma was still alive. You barely saw a customer in there from dawn to dusk. Plenty of Red Ricky's betting cronies, sure, but not a paying customer." She followed this up with a sharp glance at Luna.

But Luna was not giving away family secrets. The truth was that Red Ricky Larkspur had run Charmed at a loss his entire life. He kept his head above water by betting on horseracing. Luna had good reason to believe that Pyewacket had helped her grandfather out with his selections.

The cat had offered to do the same for Luna when she

first arrived on the island, but she preferred to turn Charmed around the old-fashioned way, with good management and an excellent head for business.

Ricky had famously never lost a bet on the 'gee-gees' – as the British called horses. His lucky bets had funded not only his and his wife's lifestyle, but had kept Charmed going for decades. But Luna did things differently.

Aware that Marge waited expectantly, Luna mumbled a reply.

"I think we'd all like to know how my grandfather did it," she said. "You wouldn't believe the state of the bookstore when I took over a few months ago. But things are different now. The coffee business has been good for my bottom line. I'm expecting to break even next month, and then move into the black."

"Good for you, love," said Marge, her sensible soul soothed by this level-headedness. "I wish you all the luck in the world."

"Thank you."

They had reached the High Street now, and turned right towards the building society above which Marge and her husband lived.

"So, this is us," Marge said, indicating a set of leaded windows on the second floor. "The far-left window is our bedroom. And the light seemed to come from that direction." She pointed towards a taller building that abutted directly onto their apartment, by means of a shared wall.

"Hmm." Luna stared upwards, wondering what she was supposed to be looking for. "And the humming?"

"Humming or vibrating," corrected Marge. "It seemed to be coming from all over, to tell you the truth. But if I had to pick a direction, I would say it was coming from the same direction as the light – from our neighbors to the north."

"Who occupies the upper stories of that tall building?" Luna asked. "I see there's a sandwich shop at street level."

"It has changed hands several times over the years. Fred and I have had families, and couples, and even singles as neighbors from when it was being rented out as flats. It was a doctor's surgery at one point. Oh, and a mattress shop."

"Is that what's there now - a mattress shop?"

"No, love. That was more than a year ago. Fred and I aren't entirely sure who we've got as neighbors these days. It's mostly dead quiet on the other side of the shared wall. We think it's been vacant for months. Mind you, we do hear the odd noise, but that might be rats or pigeons."

"I see." Luna took a step back and surveyed the whole block, mentally trying to strip away the modern signage and plate-glass shop fronts. "You don't happen to know where Barrington's Department Store used to be, do you?"

Marge looked blank. "Barrington's ... I don't think ..." Then she pursed her lips. "Wait a minute, though. That does sound familiar. I haven't heard the name in so long, I'd almost forgotten it existed. That was way before my time. It was before my parents' time even, and they were born in 1940."

"Could it have been here?" Luna indicated the tall building with no light in its windows.

"Could have been anywhere really. You want to check out the Records section at the Village Hall. Anyone can go in there - it's open to the public."

"Creepy place," said Luna.

"I'm not saying you're wrong about that. Fred and I had to go in there last year to check whether we were allowed to renovate our kitchen. Gave me the heebie-jeebies, so it did. You have to decide how badly you want to know where that Harrington's used to be."

"Barrington's."

"Right you are." Marge winked at her. "Or you could just ask your resident expert about it."

"You mean ..."

"I'm talking about Himself. Lord Whatsisname who spends all the hours God sends squirreled away in your bookshop."

"Oh, Jim. Yes, he would know."

Marge laughed. "Yes, Jim Cooke. And weren't we all surprised to learn that he's the lord of some manor some-where. And him such a tasty morsel and all. He'd be a fine catch for an enterprising young lady is all I'm saying."

Luna had held up manfully under this teasing, but at this she felt herself starting to blush – betrayed by her red-haired complexion. The thought of being an enterprising young lady on the catch for Jim practically brought her out in hives.

"If I see any enterprising young ladies, I'll let them know," was the best she could manage. "They're welcome to him."

Looking pleased with herself, Marge put her hands on her hips and surveyed the street. "Be that as it may, I don't see that we're any closer to finding my weird light from last night. If it comes again tonight, I think I'll scream. I can't handle another sleepless night, not at my age."

"You can leave it with me," Luna promised. "I'm on the case. It really helps to know where that light was coming from. And the humming too. As soon as I've found out more, I'll let you know."

"Well, you know where to find me," said Marge, preparing to let herself into the narrow stairwell that led up to her apartment.

Luna found herself giving way to a sudden impulse. "Oh, one more thing."

Marge turned away from the keypad and looked at her. "What's that love?"

"Please don't mention this to anyone. About the light and the humming and where we think it might be coming from. And especially not about Barrington's Department Store. I want to keep that all quiet at the moment. That's very important."

Marge mimed zipping up her lips. "Right you are. Mum's the word, love."

Chapter 23

"*You* told her what?" Harper gaped at Luna, fists on hips.

It was the next morning, and Harper had come into the bookstore hot, demanding that Luna tell her where she had gone after the Kwikmart the night before.

"I merely asked her to keep it under her hat for now to give me a chance to look into things."

"You merely asked ..." Harper sighed. "This is Marge Shaw, we're talking about, right? My mum's friend, Marge? Of Fred and Marge who live over the building society?"

"That's right," said Luna.

"You know she's the biggest gossip on the island, boss? Second only to Mum. They call her the village intelligencer."

"Do they?"

"Yes. And while she might not have thought much about it in the normal run of things, your telling her not to talk about it was basically throwing gasoline on the fire. Now she knows there's some big secret attached to what she saw and heard, it'll be the only thing she talks about for a week."

"Do you really think so?"

"Yes, I do. Especially now that the local spooky lady told her to keep quiet about it."

Luna pulled a face. "Not the local spooky lady."

Harper drilled her forefinger into the counter. "Local. Spooky. Lady. I honestly thought you would know better, boss. You're normally so good at reading people ..."

She broke off and gave Luna a narrow look. "Wait a minute. You did it on purpose, didn't you?"

Pyewacket hopped onto the counter and crashed his head against Harper's arm, as though to congratulate her. She rubbed between his ears absently.

Luna laughed. "Yes, okay, I did it on purpose."

"But why, boss? After all the trouble you and Jim have gone to, keeping the whole Barrington's angle a secret. You even removed pieces of the puzzle so no one else could figure it out."

Luna didn't remember sharing any of that with Harper, but she should have known by now that nothing happened in the bookstore that her barista wasn't aware of. And while Harper was as fond of gossip as the next Moonstone Islander, she knew very well how to keep a still tongue in her head.

"I don't know exactly what made me do it," she said. "Call it an impulse of the moment. It was the same feeling that made me put the puzzle out in public in the first place."

"You're shaking the tree to see what falls out."

"Exactly. There is someone walking around on this island right now who believes they have got away with murder. They're a very cool customer. And there's no evidence against them. No one witnessed them hit Paul Robard over the head and the murder weapon has not been found. They could quite easily continue to get away with it."

This didn't suit Harper's sense of justice. "Surely not? D.S. Knight will crack the case, won't she?"

"Not if there's no further evidence. There are too many people with complicated emotions and potential motives. And it's not like they all did it. It's not a *Murder on the Orient Express* situation. No, this was the work of one person. And it's somehow connected to the puzzle."

"Then the puzzle can be used to expose them."

"Exactly. If Marge spreads the news about her mysterious bright light and tells people I was asking about Barrington's Department Store, it might panic the murderer into making a move."

"Fingers crossed," said Harper. "But in the meantime, some of us have work to do." She bent down to examine the display Luna had created. "What's the cookie of the day then? Oh, oatmeal and raisin. That always goes down well, except for that first time when everyone got the runs. Didn't seem to put them off, though. Mind you, I'll never forget the face of that poor child who thought the raisins were chocolate chips. You've never seen such disappointment. You'd swear we had personally betrayed him."

Laughing heartily, Harper took up her station at the serving hatch and began taking coffee orders.

Feeling like someone who has thrown the cat among the pigeons and is waiting for the pigeons to respond, Luna went outside to check on her window display. No books had been sold overnight, obviously, but a large piece of cobweb had fallen to the ground under the weight of the plastic spiders Harper had added that morning.

Luna draped the cobwebs more artistically and stuck the spiders up using the suction cups on the underside of their abdomens. Several people waved at her from the street as they walked past, but no one stared or slowed down or showed any undue interest in the bookstore. Perhaps there would be more action later in the day.

A flash of tweed caught Luna's eye. Jim Cooke had arrived for another day of research. But it was a smaller figure in the street-side coffee queue that really grabbed her attention. Where had she seen that checked shirt before?

"Peter Pipstow," she muttered as the name came back to her.

Seeing him reminded Luna that her application to join the internet chatroom for hobbyists remained unanswered, just as he'd predicted.

Peter Pipstow might not have been related to Paul Robard, either by birth or adoption, but he worked in the same industry and knew the major players. It was time to take a stroll in his direction.

"Mr. Pipstow," she said, as though seeing him for the first time. "You're still on the island."

"Not for long." He held out his hand for the change Harper passed him and slid a few coins into the tip jar. Then he sipped his cappuccino with satisfaction. "I'm leaving on the noon ferry. The jigsaw puzzle convention is winding down tomorrow, but I've bought or ordered all the stock I want. It's time to get back to real life."

"I hope you've enjoyed your time on the island."

He took another sip and stared out to sea in the direction of the mainland. The sun was up, and a pearly glow suffused the horizon. "It's a lovely spot. If only Paul were still alive, it would have been a perfect few days. I'm going to miss him and his sudden enthusiasms. He made us all believe that we were just one discovery away from making our fortunes."

"Can I tempt you into the bookstore to work on the

puzzle for a few minutes? You made more progress on it than anyone else."

He allowed himself to be led into Charmed and ushered towards the puzzle table where he looked at the progress with interest. "Someone's been working hard. It's more than half-built." His fingers reached automatically for a piece of sky and fitted it into place.

"A few days ago, you said that the police should look into Paul's family situation as a possible clue into his murder," said Luna. "Is that still what you think?"

He placed another piece of sky. "I wasn't accusing anyone. It's just that I'm aware, from talking to Paul himself, that feelings tend to run high in his family. It's a complicated situation, with a lot of history. But I have changed my mind, as it happens. I now think that his job must have been part of it. He was always chasing after the next big thing. Perhaps someone believed he had finally found it."

Luna wrestled briefly with herself before deciding to throw another cat among the pigeons. "Are you talking about Action Comics #1?"

Pipstow's eyes widened. "Is *that* what Paul was after? That's a collector's dream, that is. There are only a few left in the world and most of them are accounted for. It's legendary. More legend than fact, actually."

"So you don't believe there are still undiscovered copies out there?"

"No, there probably are, but the chances of your average collector actually finding one are pretty slim. Vanishingly slim, I'd say."

"Was Paul your average collector, or was he more than that?"

Pipstow placed two more pieces of the puzzle as he thought about this. "He was no more than average, I'd say, despite what he believed about himself. He liked to think he was a canny operator who knew more about the business than most others, but I don't know anyone who would agree with that."

"Really?" As Luna watched him build the puzzle, Pyewacket jumped onto the table and greeted Peter with a friendly head bump. Perhaps it was naïve of her to think well of him just because her cat liked him, but she did.

"His instincts were not sound," Peter went on. "He had a good thing going with his business. He was very experienced and knew all the right people, but he nearly drove it into the ground by taking bad advice and throwing all his money into wild goose chases."

"Is that what you think this was – a wild goose chase?"

Peter nodded. "Most likely, yes. Mind you, I don't blame him. If I got wind of an actual copy of Action Comics #1, even in poor condition, I would certainly spend some time checking it out. But when I had taken the search as far as I could, I would accept that it wasn't a good lead and move on. Paul wasn't great at that part."

"The accepting and moving on part?"

"Indeed. He tended to become obsessed and to let the bread-and-butter side of his business slide while he chased rainbows."

Luna couldn't help feeling disappointed. It had been fun to believe that she was on the trail of a three-million-dollar collector's item.

"But it's like I said earlier," Peter went on. "It doesn't matter whether Paul had really located the holy grail of comic books. What matters is whether someone *believed* that he had. Because we can't discount the fact that he really is dead, and not by accident either. Someone hit him over the head hard enough to kill him. If Paul boasted to the wrong person – a fellow collector, perhaps – about what he had found, or was about to find, that could have been enough to get him killed."

"Agreed." The only part Luna didn't agree with was that it had to have been a fellow collector. Anyone would be tempted by a collector's item worth 3.25 million dollars. A simple Google search had been enough to inform her of the potential sum of money involved. The killer could have been anyone with an internet connection, which was to say, anyone at all.

~

Peter Pipstow tore himself away from the puzzle and left the store to catch the noon ferry.

Luna continued to place pieces in an absent fashion. She believed that the puzzle had already yielded its secret. Barrington's Department Store was the riddle it had revealed. To test this hypothesis, she retired to the bathroom to wash her hands thoroughly with soap and water. Then she returned to the puzzle and picked up a piece.

It tingled in her hand, but the bright glow was gone. Her hands were free of blocking charm, but the pieces no longer lit up when she touched them.

Experimenting now, she ran her fingertips all over the puzzle, starting with the outer frame and moving slowly inwards. The tingling feedback she experienced as she did so felt so much like electricity that she glanced under the table to make sure that she hadn't accidentally accessed a live cable. But there was nothing there. It was just her and the puzzle. And the cat.

Luna lifted a hand off the puzzle and stroked Pyewacket's back. His tail puffed up like a giant pipe cleaner and he made a grumbling sound.

"Oh, sorry about that. So you feel it too? I wondered if I was imagining it."

The cat rippled his fur and grumbled again. Still fascinated with the puzzle, Luna ran her fingers over it again, working her way towards the center.

The tingling sensation was strongest over Barrington's Department Store, and strongest of all in one particular spot that her right forefinger settled on. So powerful was the sensation that Luna couldn't keep her hand there. It was uncomfortable to the point of pain.

"Don't let anyone touch it," she told the cat before hurrying off in the direction of the permanent collection.

Luna could see that Jim was deeply engrossed in his work. When he got like that, a bomb could go off and he wouldn't notice. She hated to disturb him, but this felt important.

"Jim," she said urgently. "Jim. *Jim!*"

He looked up at her third attempt. "What's up?"

"Come and feel this. It's important."

"Did you say *feel*? What must I feel?"

"I also want to feel," called Harper from the coffee station.

"Oh, hush, you two," said Luna. "This is serious."

Jim followed her to the puzzle and watched in mystification as she ran her fingertips over it. "What's happening here? Now you're communicating with the puzzle by touch?"

"Well, first of all, I washed all of the blocking cream off my hands, but the puzzle isn't lighting up."

"So, something has worn off."

"Possibly. My theory is that the puzzle has already given

up its secret. But there's something else. Run your fingers over the pieces and tell me what you feel."

"Okay." Deeply skeptical, Jim placed both hands on the puzzle and brushed his fingertips lightly over the surface. "What is it I'm supposed to be feeling?"

"The tingling! Can't you feel it? Don't tell me that has stopped as well."

Nudging him aside, Luna ran her hands across the puzzle. She almost recoiled from the strength of the sensation. "No, it's still there, stronger than ever. Try here in particular." She pointed to the part of the puzzle where the intensity of the tingling was almost painful.

Jim slid his fingers over the puzzle in a circular motion. It didn't help. "Still nothing."

Luna made a frustrated sound. "It's here!"

Standing behind him, she grabbed his wrists and placed them on the puzzle. Then she slid her palms down until they covered the backs of his hands and guided him to where the tingling was strongest.

"There. Can you feel that?"

Jim's fingers tingled and buzzed with electricity, a not entirely pleasant sensation. "Yes. Yes, I feel it. Wow, it's strong."

Luna leaned in closer and released his left hand, retaining her hold on his right. It was tricky because he was so much bigger than she was, with much longer arms. "Can you feel it getting weaker over *there*," she moved his hand out to the edge of the puzzle. "But stronger over here?" She moved it closer to the source.

"Absolutely, I can."

"Sorry to interrupt this Demi Moore and Patrick Swayze moment."

Luna leaped back as Jim's sister appeared behind them.

Then she saw that his mother had also appeared and felt herself beginning to blush.

"Who's Demi Moore?" Harper had joined the party.

Bernie rolled her eyes. "Demi Moore! The actress from *Ghost*."

"What's *Ghost*?"

"Oh, my gosh. You're so young, it shouldn't be allowed. It was a classic movie from the nineties where he comes back as a ghost, and they have that sexy scene over the pottery wheel."

"Oh, I think I've seen it on Tik Tok."

Jim cleared his throat. "Luna was just, um, showing me something."

"We looked in to say goodbye," said Lady Kelvin. "We're leaving on the noon ferry. The estate won't run itself, you know."

"Of course it won't." Jim leaned in to kiss his mother's cheek and gave his sister a giant bear hug. "It's been lovely to see you both. I hope you got all your shopping done for the wedding."

Lady Kelvin patted his chin. "Not even close, my darling, but we'll be ready in time, never fear."

She shook hands with Luna. "It was good to meet you. I knew your grandfather a little and you remind me of him. He was a lovely man."

Bernie hugged Luna and pointed towards the front door where she had left Sir Lancelot's cage. "Look. They're also saying goodbye."

Pyewacket mashed his head against the bars of the cage as Sir Lancelot leaned heavily against it and made trilling sounds in his throat. It did indeed seem as though they were saying their farewells.

"I'll invite you to the wedding," Bernie promised. "You and Pyewacket. So, we can keep this bromance going."

"I'd like that very much, thank you."

Bernie winked at Luna and picked up her rooster's cage. Then – with an audacity that made Luna feel faint – she commanded her mother to stop dawdling and come along now. As the ladies strode away in the direction of the docks, Luna redirected her attention to the puzzle.

"Weird, isn't it?" she said.

"There has to be a logical explanation," Jim muttered, lifting the puzzle box off the table and peering beneath it. When no source of the electrical buzzing revealed itself, he got down on his hands and knees and crawled under the table, convinced there was a device attached to the underside. Finally, he checked the nearest electrical sockets for wires. Then he stood up and brushed himself off.

"Scratch that. There is no logical explanation. Once again, the source of the weirdness is you."

From anyone else, a remark like that would have made Luna anxious and defensive. Coming from Jim, it felt harmless, even affectionate. She smothered a smile.

"Not to add to the weirdness, but I feel like the puzzle is trying to tell us something."

"You could be right. Jim ran his fingers over the surface again. "Of course, now I can't feel a thing. Where was the buzzing strongest?"

Chapter 24

*L*una took a moment to familiarize herself with what she thought of as the vibratory geography of the puzzle. She closed her eyes and let the buzzing flow through her. "Here," she said at last. "It's around here."

Jim looked at the part of the puzzle she was swirling her hands around and shook his head. "That is too wide an area. There must be at least three shops there. More these days as the shop fronts have got smaller. Can't you narrow it down?"

Luna pulled a face. "I don't want to. It's sore."

Jim rubbed his hands together, as though recalling the sensation. "I get that. It wasn't comfortable for me either, and I was getting it at second hand. But for this information to be useful, we need to be as precise as possible. Would you like to take a break and try again later?"

Luna took a breath. "No. This needs to happen now. The puzzle convention is wrapping up and people are leaving the island. I don't want this to remain unsolved. Paul deserves better."

"Why don't you try putting on a lick of that blocking cream?" Harper called from across the store, once again demonstrating her superhuman hearing. "Just enough so that you can still feel, but it's not actually painful."

"That's not a bad idea."

Luna retrieved the remaining blocking cream from her fridge at the coffee station and brought it over to the puzzle to experiment. It took a frustratingly long time to get the amount right. Too much cream and she couldn't feel the buzzing from the puzzle at all. Too little cream and she wanted to pull her hands away, as though from a livewire. She seemed to be becoming more sensitive to the puzzle by the minute.

She finally got it right by applying a thin layer of cream and then washing some of it off with enchanted water. She didn't tell Jim and Harper that this was what she was doing, leaving them to wonder why the water from the kitchen faucet wasn't good enough and why she needed to prepare a special bowl of water in her apartment. There were some things one kept to oneself.

If they happened to notice that the water in the bowl seemed to glisten with an otherworldly shine, they didn't comment.

"Okay, now we're in business." Luna ran her fingers over the center of the half-built puzzle. Her ability to discern the strength of the buzzing was much improved. "I was right that it is strongest here." She indicated an area that included Barrington's Department Store, the cheese shop, the bicycle shop, and a newsagent.

"Try to narrow it down," said Jim. "Is it stronger at ground level or higher up?"

Luna shut her eyes in an attempt to focus. "Here." She opened her eyes to see that her fingers had landed on the second floor.

"Okay, so it's stronger above ground level." Jim made a

note on his phone. "Now, how about left to right? Let's really try to pinpoint it."

Luna closed her eyes again and focused on the lateral plane. "Here. This is the strongest point of all."

She and Jim pored over the puzzle. He took a photo of her finger on the exact spot it was pointing to, which was clearly part of Barrington's.

"Watch this nifty trick." Holding his phone out for Luna to see, he used an app to superimpose the photo over another more modern photo of the High Street. It seemed to date from the late twentieth century.

"Where did you get that?" asked Luna.

"From the records section at the Village Hall. I chose it because its proportions and plane of elevation are identical to the puzzle."

"What is there now?"

Jim enlarged the image with thumb and forefinger. "This is still the building society, with a residential apartment above it. And that is now a sandwich shop next to it. I'm not sure what's above that now. It used to be the Men's Cravat and Neckwear department of Barrington's."

"It's vacant," Luna blurted, as it all came into focus for her.

"Oh, you know it." Jim sounded surprised.

"It used to be a doctor's surgery, then it was residential for a while, then it was a mattress shop, and now it's vacant. Marge told me."

"Marge of Fred and Marge?" asked Jim. "They live over here." He indicated the neighboring apartment.

"That's right. I ran into her at the Kwikmart yesterday evening."

"She's a chatty soul."

"She sure is. She thinks you would make a fine catch for an enterprising young lady, by the way."

Jim rubbed his knuckles against the lapel of his jacket. "And so I would."

Luna suppressed another grin. "Marge says she was kept awake the night before last by a mysterious light and humming noise that seemed to come from the vacant premises next door."

"Interesting. I guess she has already told the whole village about that."

"I guess she has. In fact, I encouraged her to. I'm at that stage of the investigation where I want to shake all the trees to see what falls out."

"Then how about this? You and I pay a visit to that vacant apartment tonight. See what secrets it might be harboring."

∼

When Jim knocked on the door of Charmed at fifteen minutes to midnight later that night, Luna had almost forgotten what he was there for. She was so wrapped up in trying to diagnose the sick pot plant Ellie Granger had given her to rehabilitate that all thoughts of puzzles and mysterious lights had gone out of her head.

She sent him a text.

Come on up. It's open. I'm just busy with something.

Jim tutted as he let himself into her apartment. "You really shouldn't leave your front door unlocked, especially at this time of night. Anyone could just walk in."

Luna stared at the pot plant, willing it to reveal its ailment to her. "Someone did just walk in – you. But you didn't know it was unlocked until I told you."

"True, but with that puzzle standing out there in the open, you should really be more careful."

"I'm shaking trees, remember."

Jim contemplated the pot plant. "That's a very small tree. What is it exactly?"

"It's fennel. Ellie Granger asked me to see if could resuscitate it."

"It looks sick, all right. What's wrong with it?"

"I'm not sure." Luna tried to rein in her frustration. "It won't tell me, the stubborn thing."

Jim opened his mouth, and then closed it again. He decided to watch rather than comment.

Luna circled the plant, trailing her fingers through its drooping foliage. Then she inserted a forefinger into the soil and closed her eyes, trying to tune in to any messages it might be sending her. The problem was that the plant was so close to death she could discern almost no information from its life source.

Sometimes it was better to let a plant die. Everything had a natural cycle of life and death, and it was better not to interfere with that. But Luna had a strong feeling that this wasn't the case with Ellie's fennel. It had a will to live, however faint that might be.

She washed her hands at the kitchen sink to get rid of any last traces of blocking cream before trying again. This time, she picked up a clue as she sank her finger into the soil.

Lack of water was definitely not the problem. Ellie had watered it diligently. Perhaps a little too diligently. For the first time, Luna detected that the soil was not just damp, but soggy. The soil clung to the water in a way that suggested poor drainage. And the nutrient content was low, much lower than she had at first thought.

"Aged compost," she muttered. "That's what you need."

Fortunately, she had some to hand. Up until now, Luna had bought her compost in bags from the garden center, but more recently her counter-top composter had been turning household waste into quality compost that she used in her container garden. However, this situation called for a more mature compost than her homemade version could provide.

Luna cut open a bag that promised to contain compost aged for at least eighteen months. Using her hands and a small fork, she distributed it evenly into the small pot, scrabbling at the bottom to scrape away claggy soil from the drainage holes. A puddle of moisture began to gather in the saucer under the pot.

"There. That's better." She tidied up and washed her hands again.

"It is?" Jim squinted at the plant. "It still looks sick to me."

"No, it's already much happier." Luna had detected a surge in the plant's life force. "I'll check on it later, but I think it will be fine now."

Jim looked at the plant again. Was it his imagination or did the leaves already appear less wilted? "Well, that was interesting to watch, if a little creepy. Shall we get on now?"

"Lead on, Macduff."

"Is that what you're wearing?"

Luna looked down at her bootleg jeans and colorful

sweater. "What's wrong with what I'm wearing? I thought I looked nice."

"You look very nice," said Jim. "Just not entirely appropriate for night work."

"So ... black, then?"

"Preferably."

Luna pulled a face. "I hardly ever wear black."

"You'll survive. And cover up your ... you know ..." He made rolling motions with his hands in the direction of her head. "Glowy hair."

She smirked. "Glowy hair?"

"It reflects too much light. Your hair practically glows in the dark. And it's too distinctive. Don't you have a knitted cap you could tuck it into?"

"Urrgh, okay. I'll try."

Luna retreated to the bathroom to pull on a pair of black leggings and a black sweater. She fitted a grey knitted cap over her red hair and tucked the waist-length strands out of sight. Her scalp immediately began to itch and burn. As usual, her hair objected to being covered.

"Now, stop that," she told her reflection sternly. "It's necessary, and besides, it's only for a little while."

"Who are you talking to?" called Jim.

"My hair. It doesn't like the cap."

"Okayyy."

As Luna stepped out of the bathroom, she rolled her eyes at the sight of the broad grin on Jim's face.

"What?"

"You look like you're wearing a giant pillow on your head."

"I can't help it. I have a lot of hair.

"Well, it ..." Jim stopped talking as a noise from downstairs made them both freeze. It sounded like a heavy body colliding with furniture. "What was that?"

Luna cocked her head and listened. "I'm not sure."

"The cat, maybe?"

"Maybe. He is rather prone to the midnight zoomies." She glanced down as something collided with her ankle. It was the cat. "Except that he is up here with us."

As they listened, more stealthy noises reached their ears from the bookstore below.

"There's someone down there," said Luna. "Are you sure you locked the front door?"

"Positive. I made a mental note of it because you had left it unlocked. Someone must have broken in."

"Well, it wouldn't be the first time. Looks like my tree-shaking has caused something to fall out."

"You don't have to sound so pleased about it." Jim opened a drawer under the oven and pulled out Luna's heaviest frying pan. "Stay here while I check it out."

"Hmm. No. That's literally how people die in horror movies. I'm coming with you."

They crept down the dark staircase in procession. Jim led the way, clutching the frying pan over his shoulder like a baseball bat. Luna followed, trying to ignore the trembling in her legs. And Pyewacket brought up the rear, every hair on his back standing up like a bottlebrush.

Jim paused halfway down the stairs, almost causing Luna to collide with him. He pointed his chin in the direction of the non-fiction section. A dark figure stood bent over the jigsaw puzzle. The figure held a penlight torch over the puzzle and attempted to place pieces in the uncertain light.

Jim crept forward and the wooden staircase creaked beneath his feet. In the quiet night, it sounded like a whipcrack.

The intruder looked up in alarm and seemed to stagger at the sight of two people and a cat descending the stairs. With a muffled exclamation, the dark figure took to its heels.

"Hey!" yelled Jim. "Come back."

The figure had no intention of doing anything of the sort. With Jim in hot pursuit, it dived for the front door and wrenched it open. The next moment, the intruder was out on Beach Road, ducking and weaving between the parked cars before taking off like an Olympic athlete. Jim was quick on his feet, but the intruder had a head start and soon eluded him.

Jim traipsed back to the bookstore, looking disappointed. "I would have had him if I hadn't been carrying this darn frying pan."

Luna relieved him of the pan. "Thanks for not throwing my non-stick Le Creuset into the street. It would never have been the same again. I notice that you said 'him'. Do we agree that it was a man?"

"Yes, definitely. An unmistakably male figure."

"And look over here." Luna pointed to a card that had been left on the puzzle table.

Jim slipped his phone out of his pocket and turned on the flashlight. "Blackstone's Puzzles. It's a business card. Does that seem a bit convenient to you, or is it just me?"

"It's not just you. It's far too convenient. I think he left it here on purpose."

"How old would you say Marcus Blackstone is?"

Luna shrugged. "I'm not sure. At least seventy, I'd guess."

"That man did not move like a seventy-year-old."

"No, he didn't. That wasn't Marcus Blackstone. I think I know who it was, but we need proof before I start throwing accusations around. What part of the puzzle was he working on?"

Jim shone his light on the puzzle. "Looks like the upper story of Barrington's – exactly where the Men's Neckwear department would have been."

"In that case, I think we should continue with our night search as planned.

Chapter 25

*M*oonstone Village was no place for night owls.

Most villagers were hard-working folk who woke up early and went to bed early. Those who wanted to party the night away could be found on the pier playing the slot machines or dancing to a live band at one of the casino nightspots. The village itself was dead quiet after midnight.

A waxing crescent moon rode high in the sky, competing with the great wash of stars that illuminated the night sky. It was a damp and chilly night, with a fine misting of rain that seemed to hang in the air rather than fall to the ground. It nipped at your nose, cheeks and ears and made you long for the cozy indoors.

The streetlamps fuzzed into halos of light as they lost the battle to the thick mist.

Luna and Jim stood on the opposite side of the street from the building society and gazed up at the apartment above it.

"That's where Marge and Fred stay," said Jim.

"No lights on," said Luna. "I guess they're asleep, like the rest of the island."

"So that taller building next to them must be our target."

"The question is, how do we get up there?"

"I can answer that," said Jim. "Most of the second-story apartments are accessed by stairwells that are guarded by automatic doors with keypads. You need to know the code to open the door."

"Exactly," whispered Luna. "And we don't know the code."

"We can make an educated guess. The villagers of Moonstone Island aren't big on security. What would you like to bet that most of them have never bothered to change the default security code from when the doors were first installed?"

"And what would that be? One two three four?"

"One two three four hash," said Jim.

"No way. It can't be that easy."

He led her across the street to the stairwell that led up to their target. "Sometimes things just are easy." He entered the four-digit code followed by the hash key and grinned at her when the door clicked open. "See? Easy peasy."

"How do these people not get robbed at night? Their security is terrible."

"Says the woman who leaves her front door unlocked."

Luna sighed. "Just that *one* time, when I knew you were already on your way."

They stepped into the dark stairwell as the door clicked shut behind them.

"Wow, it's dark," said Luna. "Do we dare turn on a light?"

"Better not. We already know we're not the only prowlers on the island tonight. Besides, it's a good idea to let our eyes get accustomed to the gloom."

It felt to Luna as though that would never happen. The darkness had a tangible quality, like a cauldron of pitch that you could only stir but never separate. She knew from when she had stepped into the stairwell that the stairs were straight ahead and slightly to the left of her. She shuffled forward until her toes connected with the bottom step, and heard Jim do the same.

"I can't do it," she whispered. "I can't climb a flight of stairs that I can't see. I feel like I'm going to fall."

He groped for her hand and took it in a comforting clasp. "There's a handrail to your right. Hold onto it and use it as a guide. Come on. We'll do this together."

With the handrail on one side and Jim on the other, Luna felt more secure. And as she shuffled up the stairs, she found that her eyes were finally able to penetrate the darkness. It was as though some inner lens had been activated, allowing her to discern shapes and shadows. The longer she stared into the gloom, the clearer things appeared.

"Where is that green light coming from?" she asked.

Jim turned to stare at her, his eyes wide and unfocused. "What green light?"

"It's everywhere. It seems to be coming from the night itself."

"Okay ..." He sounded uncertain. "Are you telling me that there's a green light and that it is helping you to see things in this infernal darkness?"

"Greenish. And, yes."

"Then lead the way. Because I can see nothing, apart from the faintest leavening of grey from the floor above."

Confident now, Luna led the way upstairs. Noticing that the dust had recently been swept from the handrail, she lifted her own hand off it to preserve any fingerprints that might be in place.

"This stairwell doesn't lead anywhere except to the vacant floors above, right?" she asked.

"According to the schematics I've seen, no."

"Someone has been up here recently. They disturbed the dust on the handrail."

"Wow, you can see those details?"

"Not exactly see. More like ... sense."

"Well, at least one of us can. We should be almost on the third floor by now."

"Yes, there's a door ahead." Luna reached out and turned the handle. As the door opened, starlight from a bank of windows ahead flooded their eyes. The greenish light faded from her sight and her natural vision took over.

"Finally," said Jim. "Some light."

They stepped into the room and looked about them. It was a large, single space that one could imagine either as a studio apartment or as the display space of a store. To one side was a tiny galley kitchen with no fittings apart from a rusted stove top. An open door to the left led to a small bathroom.

The floorboards were wooden and loosely fitted, promising several hidey-holes beneath their feet. One wall had a series of old free-standing cabinets stacked up against it.

"If there is something hidden in here, we have our work cut out for us," said Jim. "I don't know where to begin looking."

Luna could not bring herself to feel excited about searching through this dusty space. "We should keep going. See what's above this floor."

"There's nothing above it, according to the schematics. This is where the light that Marge saw was coming from."

Luna shook her head. That didn't sound right to her. "No. We need to go higher."

Jim had learned not to dismiss these convictions of hers. "Okay, then let's ..."

He stopped talking as the still night air carried the sound of a shuffling step to their ears.

"What was that?" Luna whispered.

"I don't know, but I think we're not alone in here."

Another creak sounded, louder this time.

"It's getting closer." Luna clutched his sleeve. "There's someone coming up the stairs. Do you think it's the same person from earlier?"

"Very likely. Unless there are even more of us prowling about tonight. You'd better tell me who you suspect, so I know what we're dealing with."

"What if I'm wrong?" she breathed.

"Then you named the wrong person in a private conversation. The police do that all the time. Quickly!" he urged.

"Okay, I think it's Ellis Robard – Paul's adoptive brother. They've shared a love of games and hobbies since boyhood." Luna spoke faster as the noises got closer. "He is also in the hobby business. People say he was the only person Paul fully trusted - perhaps enough to tell him that he was on the trail of a valuable collector's item."

A sliver of light appeared under the door that led to the stairwell. Unlike them, the prowler was not reluctant to operate with a flashlight. They heard a scrabbling sound, and the doorhandle began to turn.

As the door swung open, Luna said clearly. "Good evening, Mr. Robard."

The figure flinched. He had not expected to find them here. Then Ellis Robard stepped into the dim wash of starlight from the windows, and they saw that he was carrying a pistol.

Luna knew nothing about guns but recognized that he held it in a way that demonstrated great familiarity and ease with weapons. The gun was not new. It had the patina of regular use and was in excellent condition. There was something else on it – something that made Luna's hair stand on end, even though it had been wiped clean and shiny.

"You, again." He looked at her with dislike. "And a sidekick, I see." He leveled his pistol at them, holding it in a two-handed grip that reminded Luna of the police shows she watched on television. He settled his aim on Jim, evidently regarding him as the greater threat.

Indignation burst out of Luna. "He was your brother," she blurted. "How could you have killed your own brother?"

"He wasn't my brother," Ellis spat at her. "He was just some kid that my parents brought home one day. Like I wasn't good enough for them. They had to go and adopt this random boy. The only good thing he ever did was to share his hobbies with me. And anyway, I didn't kill him."

Luna pointed at the gun, ignoring Jim's restraining hand on her arm. "Yes, you did. And that pistol is what you used to do it."

Ellis laughed. "You're misinformed. Paul wasn't shot. Someone hit him over the head."

"It was you. You pistol-whipped him. I can still see the blood and hair on the back of the barrel."

He stared at her in horror, his eyes flicking from her face to gun he held. "But I wiped ..." He caught himself.

"Yes, you wiped it down. But the traces are still there. I can see them, and you can be sure the police will be able to see them too when they shine their special light on it."

"That's not going to happen." He waved them over to a

wooden crate against the wall and made them sit on it, side by side. Then he pulled a roll of duct tape from his coat pocket. Holding the gun against Luna's head, he made her tape Jim's hands behind his back.

"And now I'll do you."

"Leave her alone." Jim spoke up for the first time. "She's no threat to you, a small woman like that."

"She has been a thorn in my side from the beginning. What did she want to go and buy that puzzle for?" he demanded. "When Paul came up to me, bleating about needing to borrow money to buy a limited-edition puzzle, I knew he was one step closer to the prize. That puzzle should have been mine."

"How did Paul know that the puzzle contained a clue?" asked Luna. She had been wondering about that.

"Chatter on the internet, plus an old document he had found. Paul was wrong about practically everything his whole life long, but he was right about this."

"Who made the puzzle?"

"Some collector in the 1970s. He was in love with riddles, apparently. According to the hobbyists' chatroom Paul joined, the puzzle-maker knew where the comic book was last seen, but never found it himself." Ellis flexed his fingers. "If it's here, I'll find it."

"We'll see about that," said Luna. "Why didn't you buy the puzzle from Marcus Blackstone immediately? Why wait until the next morning to get it?"

"Paul's body was discovered too quickly. One moment, he was on the ground and the next moment, people were screaming, and the police were there. There was such a commotion that the merchants locked down their stalls. I really didn't mean to kill him. I just wanted to stop him from getting that puzzle before I could."

"Marcus Blackstone had no idea what the puzzle signified, did he?"

Ellis laughed again, an unpleasant sound. "That old fool. No, he didn't. He thought it was just a vintage curiosity. And he was stupid enough to pretend he hadn't recognized Paul when the police questioned him later. Of course, he knew exactly who Paul was."

"You still tried to frame him, though. By leaving his card in my bookstore this evening."

"He deserved it."

"And why ..."

"That's enough. No more questions. Turn around and put your hands behind your back."

As Luna turned away from him and held her wrists together, he placed his pistol carefully within reach and picked up the duct tape. She thought about making a run for it. Would he really try to shoot her now – at one o'clock in the morning in the middle of this sleepy village? Would he even be able to hit her in such uncertain light?

But maybe he wouldn't aim for her at all. Maybe he would just shoot Jim, who was a sitting duck. She couldn't take that chance.

The thought of her own helplessness made her angry. The feeling of his hands brushing against hers in that familiar way made her even angrier. Fury surged in her, prickling along her scalp, gaining strength in her chest, and firing along her arms.

Ellis Robard fell back with a shocked cry. "My fingers."

Jim wasted no time. Bending double, he charged their captor and slammed headfirst into his midriff. They lost their balance and went down like sacks of potatoes. Luna grabbed the pistol from the table and leveled it inexpertly at Ellis.

"Stay down," she ordered. "Put your hands behind your head."

He cradled his fingers against his chest and whimpered. "My hands. You burned them."

"You shouldn't have tried to tie me up. Oops." Luna made a grab for the gun as it almost slipped out of her hand.

Jim rocked back on the floor and swung himself up to stand. "There's a pocketknife in my coat. Cut me loose and give me that pistol before you kill the lot of us."

Luna sliced through the tape holding his wrists, managing not to cut herself in the process. She willingly relinquished the pistol to him. Then she pulled out her phone.

"I'm calling Melinda Knight."

EPILOGUE

*W*rapping up the scene took hours.

A rosy dawn lightened the sky before D.S. Knight was willing to release Luna and Jim. She and her team took detailed statements from them, asking them to recreate the sequence of events. Her scene of crime officers photographed everything, and collected evidence and fingerprints.

Even Ellis Robard was removed from the scene before they were.

"He says he didn't do any of the stuff you're accusing him of," Melinda told them.

"I guess he would say that, wouldn't he?" said Jim.

Luna was too punch drunk with tiredness to muster much indignation against the man who had recently held a gun to her head.

"But we've got the gun, and that is registered to him," Melinda went on. "No doubt his fingerprints are all over it. It's unfortunate that you both handled it too, but I don't really see how you could have done anything else. P.C.

Cooper shone a UV light on it and there are indeed traces of blood on the barrel. We should be able to connect those to Paul Robard without much trouble."

"Are you mad at us for coming here tonight without telling you?" asked Luna, anxiety about their friendship cutting through the fatigue.

"I was," admitted Melinda. "I hate thinking that you've put yourself in danger. But it sounds as though you were looking for evidence, not expecting to meet someone, so I forgive you. And I'm very grateful for a break in the case. It didn't sit well with me that someone could commit murder in my jurisdiction and get away with it."

"And we still haven't found the thing that Paul Robard was looking for," Luna fretted.

Melinda pointed to her team who were currently pulling up floorboards and poking into cabinets. "It's just a matter of time. If there's anything in here, we'll find it."

But Luna's eyes kept going to the stairwell. "It's not here. It's higher up."

Jim sighed. "She keeps saying that. She's like a frustrated bloodhound. Maybe you should let her loose to search. We won't have any peace until she sees for herself that there is no extra floor above this one."

"I mean, I guess there is always the roof," said Melinda.

Luna shook her head. "No. Not the roof. It's in an enclosed space."

Melinda glanced at Jim and shrugged. "Sure. Search away. Just let me know if you find anything."

Permission was all Luna needed. She shot across the room toward the stairwell so fast that Jim had to jog to keep up with her.

"Whoa there, Lightning McQueen. There's no rush to see that these stairs don't lead anywhere else."

"There's a ladder to the roof," said Luna, pointing.

"Yes, there is. Do you want to go up it? There won't be much light to see by until later."

"No, not onto the roof. But is that a trapdoor next to the ladder?"

Jim shone his phone flashlight against the ceiling. "Yes, it looks like it." The trapdoor fitted flush against the ceiling and had been painted over several times, making it difficult to spot.

Luna climbed the ladder and leaned sideways to shove against the trapdoor from below. It didn't budge.

"Oof. No. I'm not strong enough. Can you try?"

Jim took her place on the ladder. His superior height and strength gave him a leverage that she lacked. After straining against the trapdoor for a few minutes, he managed to push back one corner.

"Nearly there!" Luna tried not to sound too eager. "Shove it again."

Jim worked his hand all around the square trapdoor, loosening it. Finally, he was able to slide it out of the way.

"Yes, that's brilliant. Let me up there."

Jim willingly ceded his place on the ladder to her. The trapdoor opened a small aperture into the ceiling. He didn't think he could get his shoulders through it. But Luna was a narrow creature and might just fit. He supported her by grasping her boots by the ankles and guiding her feet onto his shoulders.

"Am I squashing you?" she called.

"No, you're very light."

She laughed. "And you're very chivalrous. But I promise this won't take long. There's a kind of crawlspace here that I want to get into. Can you stand on your tippytoes?"

Jim stood on his tippytoes and pushed up on her ankles.

She braced her elbows against the dusty ceiling, cursing her meager upper body strength. With Jim's help, she managed to haul herself up into the crawlspace. Then she fumbled for her phone and turned on the flashlight.

"Be careful up there," Jim warned as light appeared in the trapdoor. "I wouldn't want to have to take you for a tetanus shot later."

"It's just dirty up here, not dangerous. I'll need a bath rather than a shot. Now hush, I must concentrate. The vibrations are back."

Jim hushed.

Luna closed her eyes and let her body feel what it wanted to feel. She ran her fingers along the underside of the filthy ceiling. The vibrations that had guided her along the puzzle were guiding her now. Her fingers touched something in the dark – an unevenness against the rough and dusty wood.

She raised her phone to illuminate the area. It looked like a rectangle of wadded-up newspaper, covered by the filth of decades.

Gently, she slid her fingers under it and pried it loose from the wood. It came away whole in her hands, leaving only a thin film of paper behind.

"I've found something," she announced.

"What is it?"

Luna blew dust off the object and shone the flashlight directly onto it. Like a palimpsest, a ghostly image appeared. It was the original iconic drawing, from the hand of the artist Joe Shuster, showing Superman holding a car above his head as villains fled in terror. She could just about discern the blue and red of his costume and the green of the car.

Decades of lying in this damp and dusty space had fused

the comic book into a solid wad of paper, more like a thick piece of cardboard than anything else. Feeling terribly sad, Luna passed it through the trapdoor to Jim.

"Here," she said. "This is what Paul Robard lived and died for."

MORE FROM FIONA SNYCKERS

For updates about new releases, as well as exclusive promotions, sign up to Fiona Snyckers' mailing list here: https://landing.mailerlite.com/webforms/landing/r4a9m8

THE CAT'S PAW COZY MYSTERIES

THE EULALIE PARK MYSTERY SERIES

Hacked

Hooked

Haunted

Hunted

Hitched

Hatched

The Time Mavericks Series

A Slip in Time

Time After Time

Time of Trial

The Final Time

ABOUT THE AUTHOR

Fiona Snyckers is the author of the *Trinity* series of young adult novels, the *Cat's Paw Cozy Mysteries* series, as well as the suspense novel *Now Following You*, the high-concept thriller *Spire,* and a literary novel *Lacuna* published in 2019 by Pan Macmillan. She has had various short stories published in magazines and collections. *The Secondhand Witch Mysteries* is her latest series of cozy mystery novels. Fiona has been nominated five times for the Sunday Times Fiction Prize. In 2020 she won the NIHSS Humanities Award for Best Novel and the South African Literary Award for Best Novel for *Lacuna*. She lives in Johannesburg, South Africa, with her family.

For up-to-date promotions and release dates of upcoming books, sign up for the latest news here: https://landing.mailerlite.com/webforms/landing/r4a9m8

Printed in Dunstable, United Kingdom

66789745R00129